From the Files of

Madison Finn

Read all the books about Madison Finn!

Coming Soon!
Super Edition #2:

Don't miss: Super Edition #1

From the Files of

Madison Finn

Forget Me Not

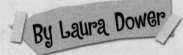

By Laura Dower

HYPERION
New York

For all of the readers
(I'll never forget *you*!)

From the Files of Madison Finn and the Volo colophon are trademarks of Disney Enterprises, Inc.
Volo® is a registered trademark of Disney Enterprises, Inc.

Printed in the United States of America

First Edition
1 3 5 7 9 10 8 6 4 2

The main body of text of this book is set in 11.5-point Frutiger Roman.

ISBN 0-7868-3768-3

Visit www.hyperionbooksforchildren.com

Chapter 1

Madison looked over at Hart's buzz cut. The locks of brown hair that usually fell across his forehead were gone.

"The barber had some kind of meltdown," Hart explained. "I asked him to cut it short and he came at me with the trimmer like he was whacking weeds."

"Well," Madison said with a wide smile, "it looks kind of . . . well . . . cute."

Hart blushed. "Nah, it looks freaky, and you're just being nice, Finnster. You're always being too nice."

"Am not," Madison said. She pulled her sweater around her body and looked in the other direction, trying hard not to giggle.

Hart blew on his hands and then ran his fingers

through the tangle of hair on top. He made another face.

"I've only been outside for a minute but my hands are like ice," he said. "What's up with that?"

Hart had on his red hockey shirt with the white Far Hills Junior High logo on the front and the number nine on the back. Underneath that, he wore a white turtleneck to keep warm. But it wasn't working very well.

The wind whipped around Madison and Hart. Instead of complaining, Madison just smiled again, pleased with herself—and with the situation. She and Hart were definitely flirting, right out there in the open, only a few yards from the school entrance. And *that* was a major step in their relationship.

A loud throng of kids pushed through the front doors of FHJH. Even though the temperature had dropped, most kids were only half dressed, dragging parkas and hockey sticks and skates behind them. The sports teams all had away games that afternoon, or at least Hart and Madison thought they did.

"Egg!" Hart yelled.

Madison saw their mutual pal, Walter "Egg" Diaz, running down the steps two at a time. Behind Egg were Drew Maxwell and Chet Waters, two other friends and members of the FHJH Junior Varsity Hockey Squad. Behind the boys were Fiona Waters (Chet's twin sister) and Aimee Gillespie, Madison's two best girlfriends.

"The game at Da Vinci was canceled," Egg said breathlessly.

"No way," Hart said. "But the buses are right here. They've been here for ten minutes."

"They had a problem at their rink. Power went down late yesterday, I guess. They tried to fix it, but basically, it's a swimming pool, and the gym is flooded," Egg said.

"Bummer, right?" Chet said.

Drew shook his head. "This stinks. I know we could cream those guys. Their team is so lame on offense."

"Why didn't they just play here instead?" Madison asked.

"Good question!" Hart said.

"Hey—if there's no away game, then what are those buses?" Fiona asked, pointing to two large buses parked on the side of the school parking lot.

Everyone spun around to survey the buses more closely. Madison saw the words MR. MOTION PICTURES painted across the side panel. She hadn't noticed that before. The name was strangely familiar, but she couldn't remember. . . .

"That must be the film crew Principal Bernard was talking about," Drew said.

"Film crew?" Madison asked aloud.

"What? Are they here to film the hockey game?" Hart asked.

"Nah," Drew continued. "I bet it's the film crew

for the documentary. Principal Bernard posted a notice by the lockers a little while ago."

"What documentary? What notice?" Madison asked.

"We each got one in our locker, too, like some kind of permission slip," Drew said.

"Oh, yeah, I saw that," Aimee said.

"You did?" Madison asked.

"Duh, Maddie," Chet said as he held up a flyer with the words OUR SCHOOL ON CAMERA! DOCUMENTARY FILMMAKERS AT FHJH printed at the top.

"D—d—documentary?" Madison repeated. She shook her head from side to side as if that could get rid of the sinking feeling she had in the very pit of her stomach.

"What's wrong with you, Maddie?" Fiona asked.

All weekend, Mom had talked about a film on which she was about to begin work. Mom and her team at Budge Films had partnered with another, smaller documentary film group and its director to produce a feature on middle-school life in the twenty-first century. One of the schools selected for the feature just happened to be Rigby Middle School, located a few towns away. Madison had been relieved to hear that the filming would take place somewhere far away from her middle-school life.

"So . . . you think they're doing auditions for a movie or something?" Chet asked aloud.

Fiona laughed. "You wish. Not like they'd ever choose you for a part."

Everyone laughed as Chet gave Fiona a hard nudge that nearly knocked her over.

But Madison didn't feel like laughing. Her brain was racing. These buses and this film crew had to have something to do with Mom. It was all way too much to be just a coincidence.

"Maddie, your face is all red. Are you okay?" Aimee asked, grabbing her friend by the shoulders.

Madison just mumbled. "Um . . . I don't know . . . I can't believe . . ."

"She's lost it," Egg said as he and the other guys walked away toward the buses. Hart approached one and slapped the side of the door, but no one opened up. Chet jumped up to get a view inside one of the tinted windows.

"I don't see any cameras," Chet cried.

"What a moron," Fiona grumbled.

Aimee chuckled. "Maybe it's a reality TV film crew. . . ."

"Don't say that!" Fiona said, looking over her shoulder. "Can you imagine? They'd come into the school and make us walk on tightropes and eat worm eggs or something."

"Worms don't lay eggs," Chet snapped.

Fiona smacked him on the back. "Oh, I forgot. You're the expert, aren't you, worm?"

Madison glanced around. From out of the corner of her eye, she saw a cluster of people coming around the opposite side of the school. Her sinking feeling grew stronger and stronger . . . like heart-burn and a stomachache and butterflies all rolled into one.

It was the film crew; they lugged video cameras, light stands, and sound equipment. One man carried a large clipboard. He wore dark, square sunglasses (even though it wasn't particularly sunny outside), a polka-dot tie, a navy jacket, and blue jeans that looked as if they'd been ironed.

"Look! There are the cameras!" Fiona said.

"Maddie . . . does this have anything to do with your mom?" Aimee said with a grin.

"Why did you say that?" Madison asked. She rolled her eyes. "Please don't go there."

"Maddie," Aimee said. "Come on. Spill it. You know something."

"Well, I think maybe they have something to do with this documentary my mom is making. . . ." Madison said.

"Cool!" Aimee blurted.

"A documentary? About *us*?" Fiona squealed.

Having spied the film crew heading in to the school, Egg, Chet, and the others rushed back over toward Madison and her friends.

"Let me at 'em! I'm ready for my close-up!" Chet cried.

"You wish!" Egg said.

Hart and Dan laughed.

Fiona went over and smacked Chet on the back

again. "Watch out. You get too close up and you'll break the cameras."

Although everyone desperately wanted to follow (and spy on) the film crew, it was getting late and after-school activities had already gotten under way. The match at Da Vinci had been canceled, but the team was due for a meeting with the coach in the locker room. Fiona had soccer practice. Aimee had dance class. Madison was the only one without any major after-school commitment. That left her heading home alone. Her friends agreed to e-mail one another later that night.

The walk back home to Blueberry Street took less time than usual. It was as if Madison had little motors on her sneakers. As she walked up on to the porch, Madison heard her pug, Phin, inside, barking. She opened the door, and Phin practically leaped into her arms, scratchy little nails and all. Madison kissed him on the head and then put him down on the hall floor.

"Mom? Mom! Are you home?" Madison called out. "Mom, I need to talk to you . . . right *now*."

"Hey, honey bear. What's all the fuss?" Mom asked, appearing in the doorway to her office, a room located just off the entry hall and living room.

"Mom, you said you'd be filming at Rigby tomorrow," Madison said.

"Oh, yes," Mom said. "The plan changed."

"What?" Madison threw up her hands.

"We'll be shooting the interviews at Far Hills now."

"You're kidding, right?" Madison cried.

"No," Mom said. "Look, Maddie, you rushed right out of here this morning to meet up with Aimee and . . ."

"Mo-o-o-o-o-om!" Madison groaned.

"The other middle school's shooting schedule fell through, and we were in a pinch, so I phoned Far Hills. Right away they said we could use the school. Principal Bernard was very gracious. He said that we could stay for a week or more, as long as we didn't disrupt classes too much. He gave us permission to interview willing members of the student body—"

"*My* student body?" Madison asked. She paused dramatically. "Are you saying what I think you're saying?"

"But it's so perfect!" Mom said. "For one thing, your school is an ideal location for the filming. You have bright classrooms and a terrific library for a backdrop. And the outside yard is just right. . . ."

"Just right for what?" Madison asked. She collapsed onto the couch, her head in her hands. "Just right for embarrassing me more than anything else in my life?"

"Embarrassing you? I don't understand," Mom said.

"Of course you don't," Madison said sharply.

"Maddie, don't take that tone with me."

Madison bit her lip. "How could you have chosen my school as a backup site for your project?" she asked, trying to sound more disappointed than annoyed. "Why didn't you ask me first?"

"I have to ask your permission?" Mom asked.

"Well . . ." Madison stammered. "Yes. It *is* my school."

"Maddie," Mom explained. "This really doesn't have to be a big deal. The crew will only be there for a week or so."

"Will you be there?"

"Not much. I've got paperwork and other tasks to occupy my time. I'll only be there to check in, once in a blue moon—"

"Waaaaaaaaaaaaaaah!" Madison wailed. "You're not leveling with me, are you, Mom? You *always* show up at your shoots. I know you'll be there all the time, and so will I, and it will just be . . ."

"No, really, this one is different, Maddie," Mom said. "As far as I know, I won't be as involved. It's the director's show, not mine."

"I guarantee that with you in school every day, this movie will become the most mortifying experience of my life," Madison insisted.

Mom got very, very quiet.

"I didn't know you would feel this way, Maddie," Mom said, sounding contrite. "But I promise I won't get in your way."

Phin jumped on to the sofa, tongue wagging. He

licked Madison as if he were playing some kind of game. But Madison was not playing any game.

"It's all over," Madison said.

"Really, Maddie. You don't have to be so dramatic about all this," Mom said, reaching out to touch Madison's shoulder.

"Oh, Mom," Madison cried. She pulled away in a huff. Madison's breath came in fits and starts, and she closed her eyes tightly to force herself to slow down. She couldn't let herself hyperventilate.

In her mind, Madison had whirling visions of being chased by—and running away from—a camera crew. Mom was out in front with the huge, Day-Glo spotlights. And when she wasn't being hounded by the lights and the soundmen, she was dodging the lenses of miniature cameras that appeared inside her locker, inside the bathroom stalls, and everywhere else she went.

How could Madison possibly endure the presence of a film crew at her school, filming her and her friends and her longtime crush? And worst of all, how could she endure a film crew led by her own *mother*?

She looked at her mother and then exploded with a rush of emotion. "Mom, this is like my worst nightmare come to life! You know I have stage fright! You know I can't do this!"

Mom stood there, flabbergasted. She tried to apologize, but Madison wasn't listening. When it came to Budge Films and Mom's job, Madison didn't want to listen to anything Mom had to say.

For the past few years, Mom's film job had caused conflict between the two of them. Of course, Madison had been proud of Mom's awards and other successes. But deep down, Madison also believed that Mom's constant work and travel had brought on the Big D. The way Madison saw it, talk of divorce had only started when Mom had started to become more successful as a film producer. Madison loved knowing that her mom was a mover and shaker at Budge Films, but she hated the times when there wasn't enough of Mom to go around.

"Are you even listening to me?" Mom asked. Madison had turned on the mute button, and Mom knew it.

"I'm out of here," Madison blurted out. She nearly knocked Phin off the sofa as she grabbed her bag and headed upstairs to her room.

Mom quickly tried to make peace by hugging her, but Madison slipped by, refusing. Phin followed close behind.

Once inside her bedroom, Madison settled back on to the assortment of colored cotton pillows and took Phin into her arms for a little doggy comfort. But after a few seconds, he got squirmy and wriggled loose from her grip. That was when Madison flipped over, pulled out her laptop, and booted up.

Brrrrrrrring brrrrong!

"Maddie! Someone's at the door for you!" Mom called out.

Madison crept out to the top of the stairs. Aimee stood there, looking up with a smirk on her face and a large bag slung over her shoulder.

"Up here, Aim," Madison called out.

"Thanks, Mrs. Finn," Aimee said. She turned away from Mom and rushed up the stairs.

"What are you doing here?" Madison asked.

"Well, I should totally be home doing my math homework right now, Maddie," Aimee said. "But when I was on my way back from dance class, I got the funniest idea, and I knew I just *had* to come over to your place."

"Funny?" Madison grinned with relief. "What?" she asked. "Please tell me. I need a good laugh."

Aimee reached inside the tote bag she had on her shoulder and produced a shiny video camera.

"A video camera? Aim, are you kidding?" Madison asked.

"Nope," Aimee said, clicking it on. She held it up in front of Madison's face. "Dad just bought this, and he said I could borrow it. I couldn't resist. After all, we better rehearse our poses before the real film crew gets involved. Practice makes perfect, right?"

"Perfect is so overrated," Madison said, holding her hands up in front of the lens so Aimee couldn't film her.

"Come on, Maddie," Aimee gushed. "Don't be

such a spoilsport. Smile for the camera. I know! Pucker up and pretend the camera is Hart Jones."

"Aim!" Madison squealed. She looked away. "I hate the camera. Stop that. Please."

Aimee gazed through the lens. "But you look so beautiful on camera. You're a movie star! Come on. At least pretend."

"Yuck," Madison groaned. "I don't feel like it."

Madison knew Aimee meant well, and she wanted to have a good laugh, but at the same time, she was still dealing with her anger at Mom. Smiling for the camera felt wrong.

Aimee flipped the VIDEO ON button anyway, unde-terred by Madison's grumpy demeanor. She turned the camera on Phinnie instead of Madison. The pug pranced around—a real ham—as if he knew he was being filmed. He planted his backside on the carpet, scratched at it with his nails, and let out a howl.

Aimee cracked up. She focused the lens. "Well," she said. "At least Phin knows how to smile for the camera."

"Aim . . . ," Madison whined. "What do you want from me?"

"Pretend it's Hart."

"*Mmmwah! Smooch!* Is that what you want?" Madison stuck out her tongue.

"Oh, Maddie," Aimee clicked the camera off. "You will never win an Academy Award for that," she joked.

Madison shook her head and sighed. After all, she didn't want to win any awards. The only thing Madison Francesca Finn wanted just then was to get as far away from cameras, Mom, and FHJH as possible.

If only she had somewhere to run.

Chapter 2

The director of the junior-high-school documentary, Julian Lodge, had all the girls in the seventh, eighth, and ninth grades staring when he stood up to present the film team during Tuesday morning's assembly.

Fiona said it best. "He looks like some kind of movie star," she sighed.

Madison, Fiona, Aimee, and their friend Lindsay Frost sat together in the middle of the room. A row away, Egg, Chet, Drew, Hart, and Dan Ginsburg sat together.

"That guy is so . . ." Aimee stammered.

"So lame," Egg said. The other boys grumbled.

Madison had to agree, at least a little bit, with what Fiona had said. Julian Lodge was kind of cute. He looked as if *he* were the one who should be in front of the camera. Actually, he also looked like what Madison imagined Hart Jones might look like as a grown-up. Both had the same buzz-cut hair and dark-framed eyeglasses.

After his introduction, Julian perched on a tall stool in front of the microphone, holding a thick notebook wrapped in rubber bands.

"He looks like he's a nice person, too," Lindsay said.

"Are we crazy?" Aimee said. "I mean, that dude is at least thirty. He's positively ancient."

"Old enough to be my dad," Lindsay chuckled.

Fiona and Madison laughed along with her.

FHJH teachers paraded up and down the aisles, passing out flyers in different colors. As they moved from row to row, the volume in the auditorium grew louder. Madison overheard snippets of other conversations; everyone seemed to be talking about the video. Julian Lodge had put the room under some kind of magic spell.

Madison wasn't sure what to think about the whole scene. After the conversation with Mom the night before, she had everything invested in *not* liking anything about the film project, including the director—even if he was cute.

At some point, Principal Bernard and Assistant Principal Goode went onto the stage to quiet everyone back down. But no sooner had they taken over the microphone than a ninth grader with

16

long, shaggy brown hair stood up, waving his arms, holding one of the flyers. Madison recognized him immediately as Larry Dooray, legendary at FHJH for causing trouble during sporting events and school plays. One time he'd stripped off his shirt during a junior varsity basketball game to reveal the school colors and the school crest painted on his stomach. Dooray didn't seem to mind being a school punch line.

"Uh . . . I know you said before," Larry stammered. "But I . . . uh . . . what is this film being used for again? I wasn't really listening."

The room burst into laughter.

Principal Bernard tapped the microphone. "Okay, Mr. Dooray," he said. "Take your seat, please. And I'll see you in my office fifth period."

The room hissed with more laughter as Larry sat back down.

"Way to go, Larry," another ninth-grade boy shouted, fist raised in the air.

Madison and her friends giggled so hard that some of the boys snorted. Madison had never seen the student body so pumped up, at least not within recent memory.

After a few more moments of confusion, Principal Bernard finally got the order and quiet he was looking for. He handed the microphone to Julian.

Julian's voice sliced through the noise in the

auditorium. Everyone stopped whispering. All the students wanted—no, needed—to know what part they were going to be playing in the great documentary-film experiment.

"Before we get into the film schedules and all that," Julian said, "I think it's a great idea if we talk a little bit about why we're here. After all, we were scheduled to go to another school for interviews and filming, but those plans changed at the last minute just last week."

Madison felt a lump in her throat. Aimee elbowed her in the side. Fiona giggled. Lindsay covered her mouth. They all knew what was coming next.

Oh, God. Please don't say it. . . .

"Thanks to the efforts of our executive producer, Francine Finn, and her daughter, Madison Finn," Julian said, peering out into the crowd. "Where are you, Miss Finn?"

Madison got a heavy feeling in her gut. Was everyone staring? Out of the corner of her eye she saw Hart turn. She couldn't look at him—or anyone—just then. She wished her seat had an escape hatch. Thank God there was no spotlight beaming on to her head. That would have made things much worse.

"Getting back to my point," Julian continued, waving to Madison once he located her. "The main reason we are here is to ask you kids a series of questions about school life. We'll film you when we do it, and the footage from those interviews will be reviewed and edited. Some parts of the interviews will appear in a short film for an educational conference next spring."

"So this isn't for movie theaters?" some kid called out from the back of the auditorium.

Julian shook his head and laughed. "I'm afraid not. This is really for a very small audience—but an important one. Everything you have to tell us is being compiled for the film and a book."

"Could you tell us anything more about the project and the book?" Assistant Principal Goode asked.

"Let's see. We're working with a special grant to produce a survey of junior-high-school behavior across the country. Your school is just one of several places where we're stopping to film. Your input is invaluable. You won't see your face or name at the multiplex, but you'll be an anonymous resource in a major study of kids your age."

Out in the audience, Egg yawned. "What a bore," he mumbled.

Aimee batted him on the head. "What do you know? All you care about is video games."

Madison and the others—including a few of the boys—snickered.

"Well, that seems to cover the basics. Thank you, Mr. Lodge," Principal Bernard said, moving to the microphone as Julian stepped back. "But, students, let's remember that you cannot participate and your footage will not be used unless your parents sign the proper release."

The sound of shuffling paper was deafening as kids searched for their permission slips among the many flyers that had been passed around.

"Okay, students," Principal Bernard said. "Does everyone have a schedule?"

The sound of shuffling got even louder.

"Oh, no," Madison groaned. "They grouped us alphabetically, like in homeroom. . . ."

Alphabetical grouping meant that Madison would probably end up filming with her nemesis, Poison Ivy Daly. Why did they always get grouped together, even though the first initial of their names wasn't the same?

"Look what it says here," Lindsay said. "*Filming will take place in either the school media lab or the cafeteria*. How boring! I was kind of hoping they'd film us at the beach or something."

"Get real," Drew said.

"Hey, Maddie, we're not in any of the same film groups," Hart said.

Everyone stopped for a moment when Hart said that. Although it was common knowledge that he and Madison were now "in like," it was still a big deal whenever he paid any kind of special attention to Madison—like now. Madison was only just getting used to it. She nodded and then looked at her feet.

Up on stage, Principal Bernard paced, tugging at his collar while Julian Lodge continued to answer students' questions. After a very drawn out question-and-answer session, Assembly was finally dismissed.

Conversations flowed right into the hall. The next-period bell was about to ring. Students rushed to grab their books and notebooks. Madison, Aimee, Fiona, and Lindsay migrated back toward the lockers like everyone else.

"I don't know how I feel about being on video," Lindsay whined. "Doesn't the camera put on fifteen pounds? I have to wear black so I'll look thinner."

"What are you worrying about that for?" Fiona said. "You look great."

Lindsay bowed her head. "Thanks, Fiona."

Ivy and her drones, Rose and Joan, walked by, talking about the film.

"Well, I know *exactly* what I'm going to wear," Ivy announced in a loud voice. "I have that little purple tee with matching sweater and those embroidered cargo pants with the buttons on the cuffs and my Keds. I just got three new pairs so I could match them to all my outfits."

Madison stuck her finger in her mouth and made a barf face, to the delight of her friends.

Hart, Egg, Drew, Chet, and Dan lumbered down the hall toward the girls. The boys bragged about which one of them would be the "star" of the video

21

shoot. Naturally, Egg crowed the loudest. He always did everything the loudest.

Aimee nudged Madison. "So wait. I'm confused, Maddie. Where's your mom? Didn't you say she had something to do with all this?"

"Oh," Madison replied, "she does. But she guaranteed me that she's totally behind the scenes. She told me she wouldn't be anywhere near the school. Thank goodness."

After the class period bell rang, talk of the documentary died down a little bit. Madison and Hart trotted off to Mr. Danehy's science class together. As they walked along, Madison felt Hart bump into her a few times—on purpose. Any reaffirmation (no matter how small or bumpy) of the fact that Hart liked Madison was encouraging.

Upon entering the science lab, however, Madison's mood shifted significantly. Poison Ivy held court off to the side of the room with Rose and Joan fawning over her, as usual. Ivy's pink cell phone was out on the desk beside her makeup case. The only thing missing was Ivy's science notebook, Madison noticed. Of course, Ivy didn't have to bring her own notes. She'd just steal Madison's notes instead.

Hart sat down in his usual chair at the back of the room. The bell rang, and Madison slid into her seat next to Ivy. The drones retreated.

"Last time I checked it was science class," Madison said under her breath. "Not beauty shop."

"Wow, you're so funny," Ivy said, putting away her makeup kit and phone. "Can I look on at your notes today?"

Madison chuckled to herself. *So predictable.*

"Why? Didn't you finish your part of the lab questions?" Madison asked, knowing what the answer would be.

"Actually, no," Ivy said, producing a blank homework sheet. "I just didn't have time. Anyway, who cares about homework when we're all going to be in a documentary? I figured that you'd let me share your answers. You know I'd do the same for you."

Madison sighed. She took out her own filled-in sheet of questions from the homework and passed it to Ivy.

"You can copy mine today," Madison said, reluctantly. "But next time, Ivy, I swear, you have to face Mr. Danehy on your own. I won't help you."

"Yeah, sure," Ivy said, quickly writing down Madison's answers on her own work sheet as if they were her own.

Madison was relieved that class went by quicker than quick. She couldn't stand sitting near Ivy Daly, or putting up with her attitude, for much longer. As soon as the bell rang, Madison leaped from her seat and made a beeline for the door.

Hart raced to the door, too. They walked out at the same time.

"I can't stop thinking about this film thing. What are you going to wear?" Hart asked.

Madison laughed. "Oh, my God."

"What?"

"You're worried about how you'll look at the video shoot?" Madison asked. "You sound like Ivy."

"Hey," Hart said, as he struck a pose and did a classic Ivy imitation.

Madison stopped short. "You know what, Hart? I think the entire school has lost its mind."

Hart had been joking, but he seemed a little offended by Madison's quips. Even so, she didn't feel like taking anything back. Didn't Hart and everyone else know that the docudrama being made was based on a bunch of boring, ordinary questions about boring, ordinary things?

"There she is! Maddie!"

Madison turned quickly. She nearly knocked Hart's book bag right off his shoulder. Then she nearly fainted.

"M—M—Mom?"

Madison gulped. What was Mom doing here?

"Hello, Hart," Mom said with a wink.

Madison wanted to die. A wink?

"Hello, Mrs. Finn," Hart replied politely.

Had he seen the wink? Mom was about to ask them a question or say something, but just at that moment a crowd of kids pushed into the hall from one of the other classrooms. It was a case of perfect timing (or at least perfect timing for Madison). Fiona and Aimee led the pack.

"Mrs. Finn!" Aimee cried. She ran over and gave Madison's mom a hug.

"Aimee! Fiona! How are you both?" Mom asked.

"We're great, Mrs. Finn. . . ." Fiona started to say. But Madison interrupted.

"Mom, what are you doing here?" Madison asked.

Mom reached out and squeezed Madison's shoulder. "Well, there's been a change of plan, honey bear," she said with a nonchalant shrug. "It couldn't be helped."

Honey bear? Madison cringed when Mom called her that in front of her friends. She felt four years old.

"It turns out that the director wants the producer on site for the shoot, so I guess that means I'll be around after all. . . ." Mom said.

"That is so cool, Mrs. Finn. You'll be in school with us?" Fiona cried.

"Wow, Maddie!" Aimee said.

"Wow? Yeah. Wow," Madison said in a low voice. "But wait a sec, Mom, you won't be here for the whole shoot, right?"

"Yes, actually, I will," Mom replied quickly.

"Mom, you're kidding."

"No, honey bear, I'm not kidding," Mom said, shaking her head. "That's the way the ball bounces, I guess. But it will be fun, fun, fun!"

The way the ball bounces? Fun, fun, fun?
Gack.

Sometimes Mom said things that sounded so dorky and so outer-limits embarrassing. It was bad enough that she said those things, but why did she always have to say them in front of Madison's friends? Why did she have to be there, at school, right now? Why? Why? WHY?

It took every ounce of Madison's energy to keep from screaming.

Chapter 3

Whenever it came to work projects, Madison always tried to be Mom's biggest fan and biggest supporter. But this week, Madison wasn't ready to be a cheerleader for Mom's work. Not at FHJH. Not in front of her friends or her crush, and especially not in front of the enemy.

After school on Tuesday, as Madison turned the corner on to Blueberry Street, she came to an important realization.

It was time for a Mom boycott.

Madison knew that Mom couldn't help her hectic work and filming schedule, or the decisions made by Julian Lodge. But why hadn't Mom warned Madison about the fact that this documentary might be filmed at Madison's school? She *had* to have known.

Phin jumped up to say hello as Madison walked through the front door. She scooped him up and whispered to him about the boycott, as if he might even understand. Sometimes it was true that Phinnie could read Madison's mind. Could he read it right now?

Naturally, Mom wasn't home. Madison had left her at the school, setting up with Julian Lodge for the next day. On the counter in the kitchen Madison spotted a note written on the back of a scrap of paper.

> M,
>   *Call Daddy. He wants to see you*
> *Thurs. for dinner.*
>
>   *Love,*
>   Mom
>   *xoxo*

Madison crumpled up the paper and tossed it across the room, missing the wastebasket. She grabbed the kitchen phone and speed-dialed Dad.

"Hello, there!"

It was Dad's way-too-perky answering machine that picked up.

"Hey, Dad," Madison mumbled after the beep. "Mom said you called . . . about dinner . . . Um . . . Thursday night is okay, I guess. Can we try that new Mexican place near you? . . . Um . . . Call me back. Bye."

She hung up the phone and poked her head into the fridge for a snack before calling Phinnie to take him for a quick walk.

When she got back from walking Phinnie, Madison went right upstairs to her room. It took only a few moments to boot up her orange laptop and get on to the bigfishbowl.com Web site. Madison had a few e-mails waiting for her.

FROM	SUBJECT
✉ JeffFinn	Burgers and Fries
✉ Boop-Dee-Doop	Ski Sale
✉ GoGramma	Knitting
✉ Sk8ingboy	Shoot

The first was from Dad, about the Thursday dinner. Madison hit REPLY and told him the same things she'd said on the phone message. She couldn't wait to talk to and see him in person. Sometimes Dad was good at helping Madison understand her bad feelings about Mom.

The message after Dad's was a coupon from Madison's favorite online store, Boop-Dee-Doop. It was their annual winter sale, but Madison knew she didn't need any more mittens or scarves. At least she didn't *think* she needed any more woolly stuff. Her feelings about that changed significantly when she read the next e-mail from Gramma Helen.

From: GoGramma
To: MadFinn
Subject: Knitting
Date: Tues 25 Jan 2:42 PM

Maddie,

How are my favorite granddaughter
and my favorite pug? I got your
nice thank-you note for the sugar
cookies. That's my favorite recipe,
too. I love hearing from you on
e-mail, but my goodness I love it
even more when you send me an
actual paper letter. I especially
liked the little cat stickers and
the drawing in the corner of your
envelope. You are so good at
making pictures and collages--even
on letters.

This week I am finishing up a little
something else for you that I've
been knitting for a month. It's an
afghan for your bedroom and I hope I
got the colors right. You haven't
changed the wallpaper, have you?

Chicago is so cold. It takes at
least three pairs of socks to keep
my toes warm these days. We've been
getting loads of snow, but I guess

that's just how the ball bounces.
It's always like that in the
winters here.

I will call over the weekend. I
love you all.

Gramma Helen

Madison reread the part where Gramma Helen said, "the ball bounces," just like Mom would have said. They could be so different, Mom and Gramma, and yet they were also so much alike.

There was one final e-mail in Madison's e-mailbox. Of course she recognized the screen name and clicked on it to open it.

From: Sk8ingboy
To: MadFinn
Subject: Shoot
Date: Tues 25 Jan 4:01 PM
Egg told me that yr mom is gonna be
in school ALL WEEK? Hey I know ur
being nice 2 yr Mom and all that
but I would DIE if my parents were
in my school so long no matter how
nice they r. Whoa. I looked @ the
sked and saw that we don't have n e
filming @ the same time. I was
sorta bummed out. Maybe u should

get yr mom 2 change that LOL. Did u
still wanna go 2 the movies w/me
and Drew and Elaine and maybe Egg
and Fiona 2? Lemme know. This wkend
hockey might go late, but we could
still do it.

C ya

Hart

p.s.: I HATE Mr. Danehy. The sci
homewk this week STINKS. I can't
get lower than a B or Dad will
ground me.

Madison smiled when she'd finished Hart's
e-mail. Lately, they'd been exchanging notes online
and had even passed a few in their lockers at school.
These were all signs that their "connection" was
realer than real. If only Madison hadn't had to deal
with Mom's movie, everything in life would have
been that much closer to perfect.

She hit SAVE.

Madison decided that any communication from
Hart deserved its own special folder, to be filed away
in for all eternity.

No sooner had she hit the SAVE key than an
Insta-Message came on to her computer with a loud
ding.

```
<Bigwheels>: Well HELLOOOOOOOO U :>)
```

Her keypal! Madison headed in to one of the regular chat rooms where she and Bigwheels liked to talk. Sending e-mail back and forth was one thing, but getting to chat back and forth at the same time was completely different—and way better—especially after the crummy day Madison had had.

```
<Bigwheels>: Ur online so late
<MadFinn>: NR im just reading email
<Bigwheels>: how did yr math test
  go???
<MadFinn>: B+ I think How was yr
  history paper
<Bigwheels>: I got a B+ 2!! Things
  R SO AWESOME
<MadFinn>: Y what else is up
<Bigwheels>: got a part in the
  student chorus
<MadFinn>: wowee congrats
<Bigwheels>: CSS>)
<MadFinn>: im so happy 4 u
<Bigwheels>: But that isn't even the
  best of the best news b/c 2day we
  did the COOLEST thing ever EVER
  in school
<MadFinn>: what?
<Bigwheels>: We got online class
  pals
```

<MadFinn>: what IS that
<Bigwheels>: my teacher signed up
  w/a class in another country and
  we all got class pals sorta like
  keypals
<MadFinn>: really?
<Bigwheels>: yeah my class pal is
  from Australia
<MadFinn>: that's so far away
<Bigwheels>: IK isn't that COOL?
<MadFinn>: what is her name?
<Bigwheels>: her screen name is
  Pinky (ha ha)
<MadFinn>: LOL
<Bigwheels>: I know it is funny but
  her real name is Amanda and she
  lives in Brisbane and she has
  three brothers and works on her
  family's sheep farm
<MadFinn>: I met someone from
  Australia once he worked w/my mom
  he was a cameraman
<Bigwheels>: N e way Pinky writes
  the best e-mails u would love her
  we already wrote to each other
  twice today in fact I was just
  online w/her b4 I knew u were
  online 2
<MadFinn>: that's cool
<Bigwheels>: WAM OMG I actually
  think she's IMing me again right

```
       now how funny is THAT? It has to
       be really late where she is right
       now
<MadFinn>: sounds like u guys r a
       perfect match
<Bigwheels>: I know we have
       sooooo much in common which
       seems so weird since she lives
       halfway across the planet, u
       know?
```

"Madison! Are you here?" Mom called.

Downstairs, Madison heard the door keys jangle. Phin ran into the hall.

"Maddie? I got some chow mein and steamed vegetables. Come on down here and let's eat."

Madison groaned. She didn't respond, because of course talking was definitely not allowed in the proposed Mom boycott.

Instead, Madison turned back to the computer. Bigwheels was still there.

```
<Bigwheels>: Maddie? Hello???? What
       happened?
<MadFinn>: I gotta go
<Bigwheels>: go! No! SO&T!
<MadFinn>: cant, Mom is calling me
       <grrrrr>
<Bigwheels>: E me 18r then?
<MadFinn>: ok I will
```

```
<Bigwheels>: LYLAS
<MadFinn>: me 2
<Bigwheels>: *poof*
```

Madison clicked off her computer. The excitement about Hart's e-mail seemed insignificant compared to Bigwheels's news.

She had *another* keypal?

Phin zoomed into Madison's room. He scurried under her desk and grabbed a chew toy that he'd hidden there. Then he trotted out again, playfully shaking the toy in his mouth.

Mom appeared at the doorway to Madison's bedroom.

"Did you hear me, Maddie?" Mom asked. "I have dinner downstairs. I'm sorry I was a little later than I expected. We finished setting up at the school. Looks like we can get some interviews and preliminary work done tomorrow without any problems. Isn't that fantastic?"

Madison shrugged. She got up from her desk and silently closed her laptop.

"What's wrong with you?" Mom asked, looking genuinely concerned. "Are you feeling okay?"

Madison bent over and picked up Phin and his toy. He was still chewing away on the end of the plastic newspaper toy. It let out a little squeak.

"Good doggy," Madison said to Phin.

But she still didn't say anything to Mom.

"Madison. Are you feeling all right?" Mom asked. She had a baffled look on her face.

Madison shrugged again.

"Is this about what happened today at school?" Mom asked.

Madison slinked past Mom into the hallway—still without speaking. By then, Mom had stopped talking, too. They headed into the kitchen, wordless, for the Chinese food.

For the next half hour, the only sounds in the Finn kitchen were the clang of forks (and chopsticks); the gnashing of Phin's doggy teeth; and the low, slow tick of the oversize clock on the kitchen wall.

Chapter 4

 Forget Me Not

Rude Awakening: Everyone around me is ready for their close-ups. But I'm not starstruck--I'm star-stuck. It is impossible to deal with the limelight when I'm feeling as sour as a lemon.

At least it's quiet sitting up here in the library before classes. Had to come earlier than early with Mom and the film crew, which meant I had to break my boycott. It was ok for five minutes until Mom started lecturing me about appreciating her position and not getting all worked up about things related to her job blah, blah, whatever. I guess the boycott was a dumb idea b/c it didn't make

Mom see my POV at all it just made her mad. But she said we should call a truce. I'm thinking about it.

OMG movie cameras sure make people do weird stuff. Apparently most of the school got in their rush permission slips so they can be filmed. No one is ever that organized about anything, are they??? Of course I didn't turn one in, I'm such a rebel LOL. Not that it matters since Mom is here 24/7 and everyone knows that I obviously have permission to be a part of this whole terrible experiment.

Teacher alert: Mr. Books just asked me to finish up and get downstairs for the homeroom bell so I better go.

On the way back to homeroom, Madison nearly collided with Ivy. There she was: all dressed up with purple lipstick, nails, and the perfect sweater. Filming had scarcely begun and yet Ivy's vanity was already on display.

Madison couldn't help snickering. As Ivy passed by, she flipped her red hair twice and mumbled something nasty that Madison couldn't quite hear. But it was better not hearing Ivy's dis. The last thing Madison needed on top of everything else was a full-blown confrontation with the enemy.

All around her, kids talked about the documentary. Fiona, Aimee, and Lindsay waved to Madison from down the hall.

"Over here!" Aimee yelled, motioning to her.

"Do we have regular classes or not? I am so confused," Lindsay said.

"Last night all I could think about was the film crew," Aimee said.

"And Julian Lodge," Fiona giggled.

"You guys! You are so obsessed!" Madison said.

Of course they all laughed, because Madison was right. They *were* a little obsessed.

"I think the boys film later today, but otherwise they—and we—have regular classes," Madison said. "I saw a notice in the library."

"I know they're filming the soccer team later on," Fiona said. "The coaches asked us to wear warm clothes. We're gonna go outside to the fields."

"Too bad it's not springtime so they could shoot a real game." Aimee said. "Hey, I wonder if they need any footage of a ballet dancer," she added, twirling around on her toes.

"Volunteer to dance on camera," Lindsay suggested. "Maybe they'll make you the star of the whole show. . . ."

"I tried to tell you there is no star of this video. It's really not as big a deal as you think it's going to be," Madison said.

"Maybe not for you," Fiona said. "You're used to all this film crew stuff with your mom. But it's a new thing for us. It *is* a big deal."

"Yeah, it's better than anything that's happened

around here lately," Lindsay agreed. "Don't you think, Maddie?"

"Well . . ." Madison didn't know what to say. She hadn't thought about it that way before. The appearance of the film crew had sparked interest and positive energy at school.

"Plus," Aimee added, "you say it's only some little film, Maddie, but what if Julian Lodge becomes famous someday and they look back at *all* the things he ever directed and some Hollywood guy sees this and . . ."

"Yeah, Aim," Madison cracked. "Like *that's* going to happen."

Brrrrrrring!

The bell rang and the girls split up for homeroom and first period. Madison had English. Although Mr. Gibbons's class dragged a little bit, there was still a palpable excitement in the air, like fizzy bubbles in a glass of soda. Fiona's, Aimee's, and Lindsay's enthusiasm was the norm today. No one seemed to care that the documentary wasn't a very big deal in the world of movies, or that it would be seen only by a bunch of researchers and school faculty members. Fifteen minutes of fame was fifteen minutes of fame, no matter how it happened.

Eighth and ninth graders were summoned for private interviews all morning. Madison watched them slip past the door, racing to their designated rooms. Madison also saw Principal Bernard stroll past the window, accommodating the film crew and Julian Lodge in their every request. Madison figured it was because Julian was building positive PR for the school. There had to be some good reason. Interview teams made their way through classrooms during morning classes, calling themselves "drop-ins." Their job was to get real footage of kids interacting in the school setting.

Even though the seventh grade wasn't yet participating fully, the building was still a scene of pure chaos.

Midway through the day, the boys headed to the lower gymnasium for their group interview. Julian Lodge was in charge of asking questions, and he'd put up a large sign with black letters on the gym door: BOYS ONLY. But some of the girls were curious about what was going on, so when Egg, Drew, Hart, Chet, and Dan raced off, Madison and a few others tagged along.

"Wait! Do we have anything interesting to say?" Drew asked everyone, before entering the gym.

"That's a loaded question," Lindsay teased.

"I know what I'm saying. I'm gonna do a rap," Chet announced.

Dan laughed out loud. "Yeah, man. I'm sure that's just what they're looking for, some lame rap tune." As the guys pushed their way through the gym doors, the girls tried to get a peek.

Aimee and Fiona wanted to sneak inside and spy.

None of the girls wanted to go to class—where they really belonged. The foursome pressed their ears up to the gym doors hoping to hear a word or two of what was being said. They could be a few minutes late for class. Who would notice them missing if it were only a for few minutes?

Inside the gym, Julian talked in a loud voice, but Madison couldn't make out exactly what he was saying. The boys laughed. Egg mumbled something. Then Hart said something. A couple of other kids stood up and started yelling. At least, that was what it sounded like.

"What could they possibly be doing in there?" Aimee wondered aloud.

"I think someone just said something about the girls in our class," Fiona said, pressing even closer to the door. "The voices are all muffled. . . ."

"Excuse me," a voice growled behind them.

The four girls whipped around. Assistant Principal Goode stood there with her arms crossed. As she frowned, a crease appeared on her forehead. "Where are your hall passes, girls?" she asked.

No one knew what to say.

Mrs. Goode shook her head. "If you don't get to class in the next four minutes, girls, I'll be seeing you in detention."

Madison and Lindsay shot each other a look, grabbed hold of their book bags, and raced down the hall. Aimee and Fiona chased after them.

"Whoa. That was close," Aimee said.

"What was she so annoyed about?" Madison asked.

"She's annoyed because school is all messed up this week," Fiona said.

"We better get to class before someone else catches us and throws us in the school jail," Lindsay said.

Everyone laughed.

Lindsay trotted off to science class in room 315, with Aimee and Fiona. Madison headed in the opposite direction, for Mr. Danehy's science class.

Mr. Danehy sat behind his desk at the front of the room, stretching a rubber band between his thumbs. The classroom was half empty, of course, since all of the boys were still downstairs at the gymnasium.

"You're late, Ms. Finn," Mr. Danehy grumbled as Madison walked in.

"Um . . . everyone's late today, aren't they?" Madison asked.

"I suppose you are right," Mr. Danehy said, snapping the rubber band. It flew across the room.

Madison dashed to her seat.

Since there were no boys present for the first part of class, Mr. Danehy decided to make it a free period—sort of. He'd written a series of science brainteasers on the board and asked everyone to figure them out. Normally, he forbade whispering and talking, but today he made an exception. The girls were allowed to work together as lab partners on the brainteasers while Mr. Danehy worked on his grade book and ignored the chatter.

Madison and Ivy copied down the first brain-teaser. They stared blankly at the words on the page.

"I don't feel like working," Ivy sighed.

Madison wanted to say, "When do you *ever* feel like working?" but instead she just nodded and said "Me neither."

"Why were you late to class?" Ivy asked.

Madison rolled her eyes. "You wish you knew," she said. But then she confessed. "A few of us went to spy on the video crew and Julian Lodge."

"Really? Julian Lodge? Well, that's surprisingly cool . . . for you," Ivy said.

"Not really. We got caught by Mrs. Goode."

"Bummer. So what did you see?" Ivy asked.

"Not much. Some of the boys were talking, answering questions. I really don't see why everyone is so into this," Madison said.

"I know it's just a dumb documentary, and who really cares about that," Ivy said, "but I still want to look good. I love cameras."

"Of course you do," Madison said.

Ivy batted her eyes for dramatic effect. "Don't you?"

"No. And I'm not going on that dumb video," Madison said.

"Huh? What's the huge deal? Isn't your mother

practically running the whole video shoot? How can *you* get away from being filmed?"

Ivy was right, Madison realized. How would she get out of being filmed when her mother was the one in charge?

All at once, the sinking feeling came back, twice as strong as it had been the day before. With the crazy commotion about the film crew's arrival and the disruption of classes and the flirting with Hart and the ongoing Mom boycott, Madison had nearly forgotten about the actual camera itself.

Madison Finn could not, under any conditions whatsoever, be filmed.

Just thinking about stepping in front of the lens made her fingertips tingle, and not in a good way. Suddenly, Madison's face felt hot, and she turned bright pink.

"You can't get out of this," Ivy said. "Poor Maddie."

Madison wrapped her arms around her middle. "I can do anything I want to do," Madison said.

Just then, the door to the science classroom flew open with a loud crash.

"Yo, Mr. Danehy," a loud kid named Vito cried. He took his seat up front.

"Yo, Vito," Mr. Danehy cracked back. He hustled over to the door to make sure that the rest of the boys moved inside quickly.

"Hurry up," Mr. Danehy scolded. "Enough time lost. Let's get to our seats, boys."

As Hart walked inside the room, his palm opened in a wave, and he gave Madison a little grin.

Madison smiled back.

Naturally, Ivy saw it all.

"So! How's your boyfriend?" Ivy snarled.

Madison's jaw dropped. Then she blushed and said, smiling, "He's not my . . . I can't believe . . ."

Ivy laughed a fake laugh. Her nostrils flared. "Maybe the director should film you two," she said. "As if anyone cares."

But that only made Madison smile more. There was nothing better than watching Ivy squirm. Even though most of the seventh grade, including Ivy Daly, knew that Madison and Hart were an item, Ivy obviously still had a crush on the boy. She hadn't given up on him yet, which meant one thing: Madison had to continue to watch her back. When she least expected it, Ivy might try to steal Hart's heart.

The classroom turned louder than loud with the return of the boys and Mr. Danehy's booming baritone as he told everyone to sit down. Madison's eyes were fixed on Hart. She watched him eagerly talking to the kids nearby and wondered what questions the film people had asked him.

At the end of class, when no one was able to solve any of the brainteasers, Mr. Danehy shared the answers with everyone. Then class was dismissed. On the way out, Madison and the others ran into a crew of people filming another classroom.

The moment they saw a camera in the vicinity, Ivy and her drones began primping.

"Get to your next class, ladies and germs," Mr. Danehy said.

Ivy, Rose, and Joan scooted away.

Hart caught up with Madison.

"You going to lunch?" he asked.

Madison nodded. "Are you done with filming?" she asked. "How was it?"

"Lame," he said. "You were so right. It's just a bunch of boring questions about what we do at school and what we do in our free time and if we hang out in groups or date or whatever."

"Date?" Madison asked, super curious. "What did you say?"

Hart gave her a cross-eyed look. "Huh? I told them that we basically hang out in a large group."

"Right." Madison wasn't sure what answer she had been expecting, but in any case it wasn't the answer that Hart had given.

"We didn't spend any time talking about sports," Hart groaned. "But Chet did do a rap."

"And?" Madison asked.

"It was dope," Hart said. "You know, Chet's a good guy. But you're always giving him such a hard time."

"You mean Fiona gives him a hard time," Madison said.

"Nah," Hart said, "all of you give him a hard time. Aim's the worst."

"Oh," Madison said. The tone of their conversation had shifted. "So what else did you guys say on video?" she asked.

"Nothing," Hart shrugged as they turned in to the doorway at the cafeteria. The big signboard out front read: MEAT LOAF, FRENCH FRIED POTATOS, BEENS, AND BROWNIES; someone had crossed out one *E* in *beens* and inserted an *A* to spell *beans*. Another person had inserted an *E* to correct the spelling of *potatoes*.

Aimee, Fiona, Lindsay, and the rest of the guys in their group had their food already. They crowded in at their usual orange table in the lunchroom. As Madison and Hart approached with their own trays, stacked high with sandwiches and fruit, the loudspeaker crackled.

"*Attention,*" Principal Bernard's voice called out. "*Your attention, students.*"

Everyone in the room stared up at the square speaker on the ceiling.

"*As you know, we have a film crew working here at the school this week,*" the principal continued.

Everyone in the room cheered.

"*However, I am unhappy to report that we've had some incidents of students skipping classes this morning, due to the filming. . . .*"

Aimee, Madison, Fiona, and Lindsay looked at one another and tried hard not to laugh.

"*Students, I want to remind everyone that the*

most important things you need to remember are your regular classes. Tests and presentations are not going to be rescheduled due to the filming. It is your responsibility to show up in the proper classes where you are expected. Thank you."

The loudspeaker clicked off.

"Looks like the whole school is losing it," Chet said.

"Even though we had permission to go to that seventh-grade interview, we got in trouble on the walk back," Drew said. "The administration wants to be helpful, but I think they're freaking out."

"Did you see Mrs. Goode?" Hart asked the table. "She looked like she was having a major meltdown when I saw her in the hallway."

"We saw that, too," Fiona admitted.

The girls all giggled.

"Get this: my mom won't let the film crew even step into her classroom," Egg said. His mother was Senora Diaz, a Spanish teacher at FHJH for many years. "She says she doesn't want an intrusion on her privacy or something like that."

"See?" Madison said.

"See what?" Lindsay asked.

"Not everyone is a camera hog like you, Egg," Madison said.

"Hmmm. Let's see. There's you, my mom . . ." Egg said slowly. "And who else doesn't like it?"

"I don't know," Madison stammered.

"Face it. Everyone else is mugging. You're way in the minority, Maddie."

"Egg, shut up! You're not helping," Aimee said.

Madison's friends moved in closer and put their arms around her for a group hug.

"You're being a chicken," Egg said.

"Cluck, cluck," Chet added.

Fiona punched him.

"What's the big prob, Maddie?" Dan asked. "You're the one who keeps telling us the whole film shoot is no big deal."

"Is it because you have absolutely nothing interesting to say?" Egg asked.

Madison threw a poppyseed roll at his head.

"Relax. You'll be okay when they do the filming, Maddie," Fiona reassured her friend. "Just sit in the back."

"And don't say much," Aimee said.

"Ask to be excused for just a sec," Lindsay said. "But then come back when they finish up their questions."

"Why don't you try not breathing while you're at it?" Egg said.

Madison wanted to believe them, but she just couldn't. By now the many reasons that she felt nervous and camera shy had taken over the core of her being. And even if she did get up the nerve to let herself be caught on camera, she couldn't possibly answer any questions with her mom right there in the room, could she?

There had to be a way out.

The class-period bell rang and everyone shuffled their trays and grabbed their bags. No one had any video appointments until after school. It was back to normal classes for the seventh grade, at least until the next day's disruptions. Aimee, Fiona, and Lindsay rushed ahead of the crowd to get out of the lunchroom. Madison hung back, and Hart came over to her.

As they walked toward the exit, Hart leaned in.

"Don't bug out, Finnster," he whispered. "You'll be great."

Madison turned and looked up into his wide eyes. "You mean it?"

"I mean it," Hart said again, louder this time. By now they'd caught up to Egg. "And Egg was only kidding around. He thinks you'll be great, too. Right, Egg?" Hart said, flipping his finger against the back of Egg's head.

"I never said that!" Egg said. He hip-checked Madison. Egg was just trying to be funny, but he hit her too hard, and she lost her balance and fell to the floor with a loud splat. Madison's book bag's contents fell out everywhere.

Her BFFs turned back around when they heard the fall. "Thanks a lot, idiot," Madison said as she scrambled to gather her stuff.

"Good thing no one was filming *that*," Egg joked.

"I'm so going to get you," Madison said.

"Me? Little old me?" Egg said. "Nah, you're chicken, remember?"

The boys laughed. In the next moment, Madison was back on her feet, chasing them, making very loud promises that she was going to find a way to embarrass Egg—no matter what.

Of course Madison knew that before she did anything else (including getting revenge on Egg) she needed to conquer her fear of being on film.

And despite the comforting words from her friends, she had absolutely no idea how to accomplish that.

Chapter 5

Julian Lodge stood in the middle of the playing field, shouting directions and organizing his crew to get just the right shot. Madison's mom stood next to him, clipboard in hand. Although it was midwinter, the playing fields at FHJH still looked a little green in places. Luckily for the film crew, there was no snow or ice on the ground, so they could do a few staged shots of teams in action. The athletic coaches had made arrangements for the team stars to fake scrimmages in soccer, lacrosse, and even baseball. The crew would film the ice rink (for hockey) and the interior gyms (for basketball and volleyball) later.

Aimee, Madison, and Lindsay had come along to cheer on their BFF, Fiona, and the rest of the soccer players. Fiona wore her shin guards, track pants, and Far Hills Rangers sweatshirt. Daisy

Espinoza, her fellow teammate and soccer pal, was geared up, too.

"We have to play really well," Fiona said.

"Absolutely," Daisy said.

"Why? It's just a fake game," Aimee said.

"No game is ever fake," Daisy insisted.

"Aim, what if some soccer scout sees the video and decides that he wants me . . . or Daisy . . . on his team?" Fiona hypothesized aloud.

"That's true," Lindsay said.

"Could happen, Aim," Madison said.

"Please!" Aimee jeered. She politely reminded Fiona that they were in junior high school. Professional soccer tournament play was still a few years—at least—away. No one was scouting seventh graders.

"Still, I want to play my best," Fiona asserted. "Being caught on film is a way to be remembered forever, and I don't want to be remembered falling on my butt."

Fweeeeeeet!

A shrill whistle blew on the field, and the soccer coaches, along with Julian, Mrs. Finn, and the rest of the crew, instructed the members of the girls' soccer team to huddle. Fiona and Daisy ran off together, a blur of blue and white, which were the team colors.

"Good luck," Madison cried out.

Fiona and Daisy smiled. "Thanks, Maddie," they said, running toward the field.

The cast of spectators clapped for the team as they moved into positions for the scrimmage.

Madison watched Julian and Mom like a hawk. They were out on the field talking, leaning close together, and whispering to each other. Were they planning something? What? At one point, they both turned around, and Madison was sure she'd been spotted. Madison quickly ducked behind Lindsay.

There was nothing fake about the game. Everyone was playing as hard as he or she could. Madison, Aimee, and Lindsay even made up a funny cheer. They were trying hard to be serious cheerleaders, but they kept cracking up, so their cheer sounded way more like a sick whale song than a real cheer.

Ooooooh, my Feeee-Yona!

"Bend it like Beckham!" Madison screeched when Fiona was going for a ball. She knew that Fiona idolized the soccer star. She'd recently plastered her wall with a full-size poster of David Beckham on one side and one of Mia Hamm on the other. Plus, Madison knew that Fiona was a huge fan of that movie about the girl who loved to play soccer.

The only problem with cheering the team on was the temperature. As the Rangers played, the sun kept going in and out behind a large cloud. Madison and the others huddled close to keep from shivering.

After a few minutes, Fiona raced from the corner for an easy goal. Julian Lodge clapped his hands.

"Great shot!" he cried as the camera zoomed in. But the ball soared right over, not into, the net.

Fiona dropped her head.

"Get up! You rule!" Madison cheered.

"Dance it back!" Aimee cried.

"You got it next time!" Lindsay yelled.

Mom shot Madison and her friends a smile. She liked it when they supported one another, even when (or was it especially when?) the chips were down.

Out on the field, Daisy slapped Fiona on the shoulder as the pair circled back.

"Hold on! Let's take that one again!" Julian Lodge called out to Fiona and anyone else who was listening. "The angle on that play is exactly what I want. Can you gals just get into formation again?"

Even from way over on the sidelines, Madison swore she could see the panic—and doubt—in Fiona's eyes. They wanted her to try the kick again. They wanted the good goal shot. But what if . . . she couldn't make it?

Fiona rubbed her hands together fast and furiously, as she often did when she was nervous.

"Let's do it again, Fiona!" Mom yelled. She raced over and took Fiona by the arm. Madison could practically hear Fiona's anxious heartbeat. When Fiona glanced back at her BFFs, Madison, Aimee, and Lindsay gave her a long-distance thumbs-up—*way* up.

57

Fiona threw her arms up over her head and arched her back. She leaned over to touch her toes and then shook out her hands. Finally, she leaned back and ran. Her sneaker made contact with the ball. It looked good.

But with a whoosh the ball careened right past the net again.

"No-o-o-o!" Fiona called out, slapping her hands against her sides.

"No, no. Don't despair. Let's keep trying," Julian cried, motioning to his team. "The light is perfect here, and it's a good shot. Let's do this until we get it right. Okay?"

Fiona looked a little defeated after her two misses, but the team applauded her, to get her pumped up. She got into position again.

"Take three!" a film crew member yelled.

Everyone clapped. Madison saw Fiona grin. She loved the attention. Madison knew that if she'd been in Fiona's cleats she would never have been able to deal with that kind of pressure.

Fiona bounced on her toes and took off. The ball rolled her way, and she moved to the side to take a kick.

Madison couldn't believe what happened next. Aimee and Lindsay missed the exact moment of impact, but everyone else saw the fall. Fiona made one swift kick into the air and landed on her back with a resounding thud.

She'd missed a third time.

"Cut!" Julian called.

Madison dashed over before anyone else could get there. At first, Fiona said nothing. Then she whimpered, "I blew it. Totally."

"Fiona!" Aimee said, coming up behind Madison. By now everyone had gathered around.

"You didn't blow anything. You're the best wing on the team," Daisy said.

"You just have to try, try again," Lindsay said. "You know the rule."

Julian walked over to the girls. "Sometimes it takes a dozen shots to get just the right one, girls."

Fiona nodded. Madison could tell she was fighting tears. She wasn't too good at failure on the soccer field, let alone failure *on camera*.

"Maddie, you were right," Fiona whispered. "This film is dumb."

"Don't think that just because you didn't get a goal," Madison said. "Because *that's* dumb."

"I couldn't get one kick to go the right way," Fiona said. "I understand now why you didn't want to be on camera."

"Why not try again like Lindsay says?" Madison asked.

But Fiona didn't feel like taking another shot at the goal.

Daisy went next. On her first try she landed the ball right in the corner. Everyone let out a loud

"Hooray!" The other forwards on the team took a sequence of kicks after that. Pleased with his footage, Julian wrapped up filming on the field within a half hour.

Mom led the team back into the locker room to put away the equipment and change clothes. She wanted to ask the players a few more questions.

Julian Lodge stayed outside. He approached Madison and her friends as they waited on the sidelines.

"Well, girls," Julian said, "you're good friends to be out here, cheering on your friends like this."

"Yeah, we are, yes, sure, uh-huh . . ." Aimee blubbered.

Lindsay couldn't even say that much. The pair of them pasted on silly grins and just stared at Julian as if he really were some kind of movie star.

Madison wasn't falling for it. For whatever reason, she didn't like him or his movie.

"Madison," Julian said. "A little bird tells me you don't want to be a part of our little film."

"A little bird? You mean my mother?" Madison said bluntly.

"Well, yes . . ."

"You have all these other students to be in it. They should be enough," Madison said.

"Nonsense," Julian said. "The film won't be the same without each and every one of you."

Madison rolled her eyes. "Uh-huh," she said, not

giving him an inch. "Well . . . I have things to do. Maybe."

"Okay," Julian said with a smile. "*Maybe* is good. See you around, then? Thanks for the first day of shooting, girls. Tell your friend Fiona she's a real trouper."

"Yeah, sure," Madison said, trying hard not to sound rude.

"Maddie," Aimee asked as Julian walked away. "What's going on?"

"What?" Madison asked.

"Well, Julian is the . . . director," Lindsay said.

"So?" Madison asked.

"So? You're supposed to be helpful, aren't you?" Aimee said.

Madison shrugged. "I am *always* helpful."

Aimee raised her eyebrows, but before she could say anything more, Fiona, Daisy, and the others emerged from the locker rooms. Since Lindsay was getting a ride home from her dad and Fiona was meeting Chet and her parents back in front of the school, Madison and Aimee had made a plan to walk home from school together.

The air wasn't as warm now as it had been when the sun was way up high in the sky. Now it felt more like a typical February evening. Madison zipped up her hoodie and buttoned her jacket right up to the neck. Aimee wrapped two scarves around her neck. One of them was a striped one that Madison's grandmother had knitted for Aimee the year before. Madison had almost the same one, knitted with different colored yarns.

"Maddie, are you feeling okay?" Aimee asked as soon as she had the chance. "Ever since the film crew arrived you haven't been acting the same, and it's starting to bug me out."

Madison kicked at a rock on the sidewalk. "I just don't like being on camera. You know."

"But you aren't on camera, Maddie. You haven't been on camera once yet."

"I guess you're right. . . ."

"Hey, come over to my house," Aimee said. "We can study—or maybe do our nails. Mom picked up this organic nail polish for me."

"Organic nail polish?"

"Not tested on animals," Aimee said. "And it smells good, not like chemicals."

"But I don't have nails," Madison chuckled. "I've chewed them down to nubs in the last two days."

Despite her lack of nails, Madison realized that heading over to Aimee's house was a great idea. It was the best way to avoid Mom, at least for a little while. She decided to tag along.

As Madison and Aimee walked into the Gillespies' hall, they heard the clang of metal pots. Mr. and Mrs. Gillespie were scooting around inside the kitchen, stewing at least three different crocks full of what they called Vegetable Mulligatawny.

That night, Mr. Gillespie was hosting a potluck book-group supper at his Cyber Cafe and bookstore.

"Well, hello, you two!" Mrs. Gillespie said cheerily when she saw the kids.

"You're still cooking?" Aimee asked. Her parents had been at it all day.

Aimee grabbed a handful of vegan nut cookies from the kitchen counter, and she and Madison headed in to the next room.

Aimee's brothers were hardly ever inside the house at the same time anymore. But Madison found three of them there today. Roger, Dean, and Doug were sprawled across the two sofas and chairs in the den.

"What are you guys doing here?" Aimee asked when she saw them.

"Blame Dad," Roger said simply. He was the oldest brother. He helped his dad part-time at the bookstore.

"Yeah, Dad got all of us to go to this stupid thing at the bookstore tonight," Dean said. "Me and Doug have to run the food table. How bad is that?"

"Where's Billy?" Madison asked, wondering where Aimee's fourth brother was hiding.

"He had something to do at the college and couldn't come home," Roger said, "but of course Dad asked him anyway—twice."

"Aren't you helping out, Aimee?" grumbled Aimee's ninth-grade brother, Doug. He was always complaining that Aimee got special treatment because she was the only girl in the house other than Blossom, the Gillespies' female basset hound.

"I guess I'll help out," Aimee shrugged. "Dad probably figured he'd just drag me in at the last minute as usual."

"Yeah, right," Doug said. "But you'll probably find some reason not to come, knowing you."

"Even if Aimee can't go . . . I can come," Madison piped up.

"Oh, Maddie, you don't have to come. It's so dumb, and it goes on forever, and you don't want to be there. Trust me on this one," Aimee said.

They sat around talking for a while longer, until Aimee and her brothers had to go. Madison said, "Later, alligators," and headed home alone.

The inside of Madison's house looked dark from the outside. But after she opened the door, flicked on the light, and got a quick smooch and nuzzle from Phin, Madison felt a lot better. She plopped down on to the living-room sofa and waited patiently for Mom's return. The orange laptop was good company. Madison opened another new file.

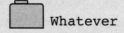 Whatever

    We sat around at Aim's house talking
about the documentary for like an hour. Her
brothers think it sounds cool. Of course

they would. Roger wanted to know what kinds
of questions the director and his crew were
asking. Doug was acting above it all, as
usual. Apparently his class of guys in the
ninth grade got interviewed this afternoon
and Doug said it was the dumbest thing he'd
ever done. Of course he exaggerates all the
time. I know he probably combed his hair
and posed for the camera. He's so full of
himself sometimes.

Unlike me. I know I sound like a broken
record but I just don't know HOW I'm going
to face the whole movie crew tomorrow.
That sinking feeling is back AGAIN. I
think b/c my Mom is in charge Julian Lodge
is going to hunt me down until he films
me. Help.

Rude Awakening: Why do I always end up
in the middle of everything, including my
very own midlife, well, middle-school-life,
crisis?

Maybe I should e-mail Hart about what
happened. I wonder what he'd say? It seems
so weird that we E each other now. That's
such a MEGA step.

BTW: I haven't gotten another e-mail
from Bigwheels yet since we chatted on
bigfishbowl this wk. Why has she not
written when she said she would write? I
guess she's busy with her new class pal.

Whatever.

Out of the corner of her eye, Madison saw Phin

jump up. She heard the sound of keys in the lock, only the door wasn't locked.

"Rowwowooooorrooo!" Phin howled.

"Maddie, you left the front door unlocked," Mom called out. "Where are you, honey bear?"

Madison hit SAVE and clicked her laptop shut.

"In here," Madison yelled.

"Oh, hello," Mom said, appearing in the door-way to the living room. "Sorry I took so long. You want to order in?"

"I guess," Madison said unenthusiastically.

Madison secretly wished she were having dinner over at Dad's. At least he liked to cook. The only time Mom ever seemed to cook was when she wasn't busy working on some film project. Madison wondered if Mom's job wasn't a hazard to their digestive systems. How much pizza and take-out Chinese could one family take? They'd ordered out three times already that week.

Mom called Lotus Queen for dinner. Then she dumped a bag of videotapes onto the living-room sofa adjacent to her office.

"What are those?" Madison asked.

"B-reels," Mom said.

"Be what?" Madison asked.

"B-reels. It's the complete footage from the video shoots," Mom answered. "We look at everything and edit down to the good parts. Julian had copies made of all the footage so I could take a look."

"Everything? Madison asked. She could read the labels on the tops of the cassettes, but she had no idea how to decode the numbers.

"Yup, there's usually hours of filming that gets whittled down to a few key moments for each film," Mom said. "But you know this! You've seen my B-reels before. Remember when we sat and watched that gorilla footage for more than a week?"

Madison laughed. She did remember.

"And remember the rain forest tapes? Half of them were blurred from the camera malfunction. What a disaster."

"Yeah, I remember that, too," Madison said.

Mom and Madison sat together in the living room for at least twenty more minutes talking about Mom's job. Madison realized, as they sat there, that maybe she was being too harsh. Mom's devotion to the documentary film business wasn't all bad. After all, Mom did get to travel to some cool places, like the Galapagos Islands. And Mom had collected some very cool stories over the years, like the ones about the gorillas and the rain forest.

In spite of their momentary couch-bonding and the rush of memories about all the great things Mom *was* doing, however, it was still hard to forget all those other things Mom *wasn't* doing.

The doorbell rang. The takeout delivery guy was there.

Madison braced herself for another night of flat noodles, soy sauce in little packets, and frazzled nerves.

Tomorrow was another day, but unfortunately it was another day with the film crew and Mom and Julian Lodge.

How would Madison ever survive the rest of the week like this?

Chapter 6

Thursday morning, Madison rubbed the sleep out of her eyes earlier than usual. She'd tossed and turned all night.

Mom was up early, too. She looked more dressed up than usual, in tailored black pants and a crimson-colored, chenille turtleneck sweater. Mom moved around the kitchen as if she were walking on air, even though she was wearing high-heeled boots.

Madison had gotten a little dressed up herself, just in case the camera did catch her in action today. If she had to be filmed at all, at least she'd get filmed wearing something cute. Her sandblasted blue denim looked good in any light, at any angle. She stuffed the cuffs inside a new pair of brown sheep-skin boots with some of the sheepskin showing on the outside.

"I see you're ready for today," Mom said. "You look just darling in that top. It's new, right?"

Madison wore a fuschia-colored sweater set that she'd ordered from the Boop-Dee-Doop site. It was trimmed with spangles and buttons threaded with silver. It matched Madison's pink button-down coat and the striped scarf that Gramma Helen had made for her a while back.

"Maddie, I don't think I say it enough," Mom said, "but I am terribly proud of you. And now that I'm inside your school on a daily basis, I can be proud of you all the time. I feel lucky."

"Lucky?" Madison repeated flatly. "Sure thing, Mom. Me, too." She was lying through her teeth. She didn't feel like contradicting Mom that early in the morning; not when she knew that she'd be seeing Mom all day long in different parts of the school.

That week, Mom was like the human equivalent of cooties. Madison just couldn't shake her—no matter what she said or did.

They drove to school and walked into the school building together. Mom actually followed Madison to her locker before finally (finally!) saying goodbye and heading off to meet with Julian and the crew. Madison went off to class, happy to be free at last.

Where were her friends when she really needed them?

On the way to first period, Madison stopped in to Mrs. Wing's computer classroom. Egg, Drew, and

Lance, another kid from their class, sat at monitors, typing madly.

"Madison!" Mrs. Wing cried when she saw her at the doorway. "I was hoping you might come around this morning. Long time no see."

"Maddie, we have news," Drew said.

"*Great* news!" Egg declared.

"What is it?" Madison asked.

"Julian Lodge wants to do a special feature on technology," Egg said. "He's going to film, here in the computer lab. How cool is cool?"

"Cool is cool," Madison said blankly, not really knowing what that meant.

"Translation, Finn: they want to film us," Lance added.

"Oh?" Madison said.

"It's strictly voluntary," Mrs. Wing said gently. "Although I would love for you to take part. You're such an integral part of our Web team."

Madison felt overcome with queasiness. "I don't know," she said to Mrs. Wing. "I think I might be busy then."

"We haven't even told you what time they're filming," Egg interjected.

"Time? Oh. Well . . ."

"Maddie, you can't just blow off all the interviews. You do want to be a part of the documentary, don't you?" Drew asked.

Madison shrugged.

"Maybe Madison is more of a behind-the-scenes person," Mrs. Wing said.

The four of them gathered around Drew's monitor to check out his colorful, upgraded, and revised version of the school's home page. He'd added an audio track of the school song, along with new graphics that all of the students in Mrs. Wing's class had been developing for weeks.

"I don't care how small this movie is," Egg said. "Our school is going to be semifamous when people watch."

Mrs. Wing marveled over the new home page, gushing with compliments, although she had a few adjustments to recommend, too. Drew clicked a few keys and started to rework a few of the graphics, but he quickly ran out of time. Classes were about to begin.

A bell rang in the hall. But it sounded unfamiliar.

"What was that?" Madison asked aloud.

"Yeah, what happened to the regular bell?" Lance asked aloud.

"The video crew tested some different bell tones," Egg explained. "At least, that's what my mother told me. Apparently, last night that Julian director guy tried some different bell tones. This was the one he liked best. My mom thinks he's a little bonkers. She thinks this film is disrupting everything about school. I mean, can't he just dub in some other bell sound when the flick is done?"

Madison nodded. "Yeah. Dub."

"Bell tones, shmell tones," Mrs. Wing said. She shooed everyone out of the computer lab. "Get to class, kids. Things are crazy enough around here. Let's try to keep to the routine as much as possible."

Madison, Egg, Drew, and Lance walked into the hall. It was hard not to get knocked around as people shuffled from place to place, not looking (or, seemingly, caring) where they went.

Since they were headed for different classes, Madison let the boys run ahead, as she stopped to adjust her pants cuffs. Although it was a chilly February day outside, her feet felt a little sweaty in the boots she'd worn. She laughed at herself. In trying to wear an outfit that would make her feel good—and filmable—Madison had unwittingly chosen clothes that made her feel absolutely, and literally, uncool.

The noise in the halls died down. The second bell was about to ring, but Madison couldn't spot any of her BFFs. She heard familiar voices just around the corner.

"We need to talk," the voice said.

"Absolutely, sir," another voice said.

Madison knew immediately whose voices she was hearing. Principal Bernard was speaking to Julian Lodge. That much Madison knew. What were they speaking about?

She adjusted her pants a little more at the

bottoms but didn't stand up all the way. Staying crouched was a better position from which to eavesdrop.

"Perhaps we should step into my office to discuss this," Principal Bernard said. Julian Lodge didn't respond at first. Madison could only hear snippets of what they were saying. She figured they must have turned to face the opposite direction.

"You know we love your being here, your using Far Hills Junior High as one of your locales," Principal Bernard went on. "But the school has its rules."

"I understand, Mr. Bernard," Julian said in that smooth voice he always used. Madison could almost see his face, smiling wide. He never stopped smiling.

"We need to scale back on the disruptions," Principal Bernard said. "I know I promised you assemblies and chances to get the student body together for a dialogue as a large group. But that will be impossible now."

"Impossible? Why?" Julian asked.

Madison's legs felt tingly. Her limbs were falling asleep. She was afraid she might tip over, but she couldn't stand up, not yet. This was too interesting. Was Julian Lodge in trouble? This was good.

Principal Bernard had a whole list of complaints. Madison listened as he rattled them off. He didn't like the camera crew following students down the halls. He had caught sound-crew members smoking outside the school. The crew left the cafeteria a mess

after shooting in there for only an hour. The interviews with students were taking up too much class
time. That seemed to be the principal's biggest com-
plaint.

"I can't have student life totally disrupted,"
Principal Bernard said aloud. Madison didn't hear a
response from Julian Lodge—at least not right away.
She sensed his frustration, however, even from
around the corner.

"Mr. Bernard . . . er, Principal Bernard . . . the stress-
ful part of the shoot is always the beginning. . . ."

Madison tried hard not to laugh out loud. Mom
had always told Madison the opposite. She believed
that the hardest part of making any documentary
was at the end—making sure the final shots were in
place. Julian was sweet-talking Principal Bernard.
She knew it.

"I realize there have been some disruptions,"
Julian said.

"Some of our students, normally good students,
have been skipping classes," Principal Bernard said.

"I can understand, sir," Julian said. "But this
won't last more than one week. Surely we can work
out some compromise in that time. . . ."

There was more chatter, but Madison couldn't
hear all of it, thanks to a generator that clicked on
and drowned out the two voices. When the generator kicked off again a moment later, Madison heard
the soft sound of hands slapping. Shaking?

Someone sneezed, but it wasn't around the corner. It was right nearby. Madison looked up and saw Hart standing there. And as soon as she caught his eye, Madison toppled right over like a pile of blocks. She couldn't believe how clumsy she'd been lately.

"How long have you been there?" Madison whispered.

"Long enough to see the truth," Hart said softly.

"The truth?"

"You're a spy, aren't you?" Hart said. But then he started to laugh—loudly.

Madison got herself up. Her legs wobbled, so she couldn't move fast.

"Shhhh!" she said, motioning for Hart to be quiet.

But it was too late. Principal Bernard whipped around the corner.

"Mr. Jones? Ms. Finn?" Principal Bernard said.

Then Julian Lodge poked his head around the corner.

"Madison!" Julian said. "Just the person I wanted to see."

Principal Bernard shook his head. "This is exactly the kind of infraction I am talking about," he said to Julian, sounding a lot more like Julian's scolding principal than his colleague in the project. Then he turned back to Madison and Hart with a shake of the head.

"You two need to report to after-school detention today," Principal Bernard said.

Hart and Madison's eyes bugged out. "Detention?"

Madison had never even come close to being in detention before. She'd never gotten below a B. She'd never even been reprimanded, in class or anywhere else at FHJH.

"Detention," Principal Bernard repeated coldly. "I need to start restoring order around here. You need to get to your classes along with everyone else in school. Maybe this will teach you. I know it will be an example to some of the other students who are pulling the same tricks."

"Tricks?"

Madison swallowed hard. She and Hart must have had the same stunned looks on their faces.

"*Ahem.* Dismissed," Principal Bernard said, clearing his throat. He spoke to them as if they were doing army drills. Then he motioned for Julian to walk down the hall with him—away from Madison and Hart.

As soon as Principal Bernard and Julian disappeared, Madison and Hart ambled, still stunned, down the hall to class. Despite all of Principal Bernard's warnings, however, they did not hurry. They loped along in a fog.

"Detention?" Hart repeated. "I can't believe this happened. I never should have stopped to say hello to you."

"I guess not," Madison said.

"Why didn't you tell me that you were listening

to Principal Bernard? Didn't you know he'd discover you?"

"No, I didn't," Madison said. She hated the tone in Hart's voice, and the clank of the word *detention* echoed inside her head.

Mom would freak when she found out.

The rest of the day at school was packed with more interviews with Julian Lodge and the crew. Of course, Madison didn't take part. She heard about it secondhand. She spent her after-school time staring at the clock in the detention room, waiting for four o'clock, along with some of the other junior high degenerates. No one talked to anyone else in detention. Hart sat clear across the room from Madison. He seemed to be getting angrier by the moment.

Madison's friends came to pick her up when detention ended. Hart said hello to the girls but then scurried away.

"What happened?" Aimee asked, sounding both shocked and a little impressed.

"I didn't get to class on time. I was hanging in the hallway," Madison said. "And then Hart stopped to talk, and he got caught. . . ."

"Whoa, you're bad," Lindsay said, giggling. "I love it."

"But you never get in trouble," Fiona said, sounding more concerned than the others. "Is something wrong?"

Madison shrugged. "Can we talk about some-thing else, please? Tell me about the filming. What kind of stuff did they ask you?"

Aimee, Fiona, and Lindsay explained how they—and other girls in the seventh grade—had been given pieces of paper listing dozens of simple ques-tions. Madison eyed one of the pink questionnaires. She thought hard. What would her answers to these questions have been?

What's your definition of peer pressure?
Where do you go to have fun after school or
*   on weekends?*
What are the cliques in your school?
What is the workload in seventh grade?
Who is your favorite teacher and why?

After she skimmed the questions, Madison turned to Aimee. "Aren't those questions kind of personal?" she asked.

Aimee nodded. "Yeah, but even though a camera was there, it wasn't weird talking about personal stuff."

"I told them my favorite teacher was Ms. Ripple, because she's really easy on grades," Fiona added, speaking about her science teacher. "I hope that footage doesn't get selected. What if Ms. Ripple sees it?"

Madison laughed. "Ms. Ripple doesn't care."

"Maddie, don't you think your mom will think it's weird when she realizes that you have not yet been on camera—especially after today?"

Madison shrugged again. Her head felt ready to explode with all of the things that had happened in the past week.

"Hart's mad at me," Madison said.

"He is not," Fiona shot back. "He never gets mad."

"Well, he got mad at me," Madison said.

"So? It'll blow over," Lindsay said. "That's how it works, right?"

Madison wasn't so sure.

"What did you answer when they asked the question about school cliques?" Madison asked.

Aimee, Fiona, and Lindsay all laughed at the same time.

"You should have seen Ivy," Aimee said to Madison. "She sat there the whole time in a manic panic, answering like she was on some kind of soap opera, waving her arms around, showing off. Truly pathetic."

Lindsay laughed. "Pathetic, but funny. She reapplied her lip gloss like, thirty times."

"And when they finally put the camera on Ivy's face . . ." Fiona cut herself off and the three girls burst into guffaws.

"What's so funny?" Madison asked.

"The camera broke!" Aimee cried.

"What? No way!" Madison said.

"Yes, way!" Lindsay said with a snort. "Well, they ran out of film. That was the official problem. But filming stopped, and Ivy was not pleased."

"Carmen, Beth, Daisy, and even Hilary Klein burst out laughing. Ivy was so mortified," Aimee said.

"The drones couldn't even brush it off," Fiona said. "It was brutal."

"Face it," Aimee said. "It was great."

Madison grinned. She tried to imagine Ivy's expression at the exact moment when the camera malfunctioned. Madison had seen that look so many times before—slackened jaw, squinty eyes, accompanied by a wild flip of the hair.

"I wish you could have been there, Maddie," Lindsay said.

"Me, too," Madison nodded. She chewed the inside of her lip.

Up until that very moment, Madison had been wearing her short after-school detention stint as a badge of honor. But after hearing about how the film crew had so perfectly embarrassed Ivy in front of everyone, Madison became sad. She didn't want to be on the outside of things—not that much. She couldn't be forgotten while everyone else got their moments in the spotlight. She couldn't afford to miss another Ivy dis.

And for the first time since Julian and the documentary team had arrived at FHJH, Madison wanted—no, needed—to be a part of the action.

Chapter 7

"Mom said that after tonight's dinner I'm grounded," Madison told Dad as they sat together in Casey's Burger Shop for dinner. She nibbled on the end of a crispy french fry.

"She'll get over it by tomorrow," Dad said. "I'll talk to her. After all, it was a onetime thing. And there *are* extenuating circumstances."

Dad winked.

Madison smiled.

Dad always understood. Or at least he tried. Sometimes Mom got so bogged down by her work that she didn't find time to listen to Madison's side of the story. That's what had happened with the incident at school. Mom had only heard about detention from Principal Bernard, and by the time she got back home, steaming like a teakettle, she didn't even want to hear Madison's defense.

"Don't worry, Maddie. I promise I'll talk to your mother about it," Dad said, taking a sip of his milk shake. "You know how she gets. She feels bad sometimes. That's the reason she overreacts."

"Feels bad about *what*?" Madison asked.

"You know. Because she's too busy. I know how it is."

"You do?"

Madison popped another fry into her mouth and chewed slowly, thinking hard about what Dad was saying.

"So, tell me, what else is going on at school besides the torture of having Mom around?" Dad joked.

Madison laughed, a little relieved to change the subject.

"Well, I aced that English test. The oral presentation was fine. I remembered everything I was supposed to, thanks to the tips you gave me. Didn't even need to use the file cards I wrote out."

"Glad to hear it," Dad said, raising his palm for a high five. "You're getting a lot braver these days about getting up in front of people, aren't you?"

"Well, I wouldn't go that far. . . ." Madison said.

"I'm sure you're a great speaker."

"Oh, Dad," Madison said, playfully swatting Dad's arm. "Where's Stephanie tonight?"

"Work. She works hard, too. We all do, I guess. Sorry about that."

"You don't have to apologize," Madison said.

"How's that boy you like? What's his name— Bart? No, Hart, right?"

Madison smiled. "He's okay."

Thankfully, Dad didn't press for more specifics. He switched subjects.

"How's Phinnie?" Dad asked.

"Hungry!" Madison said. "He ate another slipper this week. I don't know what his problem is."

"Hmmm. Maybe he's lonely," Dad said. "You know, most dogs need a lot of attention and love. And it sounds like you and Mom have been out of the house a lot, so . . ."

"Yeah, I guess we haven't really been paying attention to him," Madison said, instantly feeling a little bit guilty. Usually, Mom worked at home most days; so she could take afternoon walks with the dog. Sometimes after school Madison would take him to the dog run in the park. But now that Mom was coming to FHJH each day and Madison was try- ing hard to keep away from Mom and home, Phin was getting shortchanged.

When the meal was done, the waiter brought over a big slab of Madison's favorite chocolate cake, slathered in whipped cream. She and Dad sat there together for a few more minutes. Madison was grateful for a little bit of silence. For the first time all day, she didn't feel stressed out about the film shoot, or Mom's presence, or saying the right or wrong thing. It was enough just to *be* with Dad right now.

After a long good-bye when Dad dropped her off, Madison came into the house. She expected Phinnie to rush the door as he always did.

"Phin!" Madison called out.

But he didn't come.

Mom called out from her office. "We're in here, honey bear, still working. Be out in a few minutes."

Madison was surprised by the sound of Mom's voice. She seemed in a completely different mood than she had been just a few hours earlier. Had Mom gotten over the whole grumpy grounding thing already? Madison thought about poking her head into Mom's office—just to say hello and make sure that angry Mom was gone—but she headed directly upstairs instead.

Her orange laptop sat on the bed, still open from earlier that day. Madison had forgotten to log off before heading out with Dad for dinner. It beeped loudly—a reminder signal telling Madison to check her e-mail. The bigfishbowl.com e-mailbox flashed pink. Madison had two e-mails.

FROM	SUBJECT
✉ Dantheman	Clinic Help L8R
✉ Bigwheels	My Class Pal!!!

She opened Dan's first.

```
From: Dantheman
To: MadFinn
Subject: Clinic Help L8R
Date: Thurs 27 Feb 3:17 PM
```
OK major emrgncy here WE HAVE SEVEN
PUPPIES!!! Lady Marmalade cocker
spaniel finally had her pups today
my Mom asked me to help her contact
some voluntrs to come in this wkend
if u can. We need xtra help. Can u
come? Lemmeknow. Bye. Dan.

Madison hit REPLY and sent Dan a great big
"Yessssss!" message. She couldn't wait to help out
with the new pooches. The cocker spaniel in question was an abandoned dog that came into the
clinic pregnant with pups. Dan's mother Eileen and
Dr. Wing, the main veterinarian at the clinic, decided
they would care for the dog. Everyone named her
Lady Marmalade because she had orange fur on her
face, as if she'd taken a big lick of marmalade. It was
also the name of a crazy song from the 1970s that
was playing on the radio when Lady M was discov-
ered.

After sending her message, Madison moved on
to Bigwheels's e-mail, but she had another one of
her sinking feelings about this one. The subject line
of the e-mail was a giveaway.

From: Bigwheels
To: MadFinn
Subject: My Class Pal!!!
Date: Thurs 27 Feb 3:29 PM

U would not believe how totally cool it is to have a class pal, Maddie, it is THE BEST EVER. My class pal's from Australia, writes so dif. than we do. U would

Madison clicked DELETE without finishing the note and without realizing what she was doing. The e-mail vanished. Madison stared at the blank screen as Bigwheels's words echoed in her mind. The Australian keypal . . . er, class pal . . . sounded cooler than Madison could ever hope to be.

Madison stood up abruptly from her laptop, needing a change of scenery. Distraction was key right now. Madison figured a snack might do the trick. She marched down into the kitchen for a chocolate-covered granola bar.

Downstairs, there seemed to be commotion, or at least talking, coming from Mom's office. Madison edged closer to the door and leaned in for a listen.

The voice sounded familiar.

"When I got into the honors society, I thought it was pretty cool. I was proud. And my parents thought it was a major achievement. Except my friends, well they . . . It's not so cool to be too smart.

I get called names like Gecko, which is like 'geek,' only worse. And no girls even talk to me."

Madison listened closer. Was that Ben Buckley?

Her BFF Aimee had only recently admitted having a major crush on Ben. Madison couldn't believe what she was hearing. Didn't Ben know how Aimee felt? How could he say that no girls ever talked to him?

Madison inched closer to Mom's office door. She heard the loud buzz and squeal of Mom's editing and audio equipment.

Then she heard a few more familiar voices. First there was Lance, the guy from computer class; then there was Brendan Lo talking about math class, Montrell Morris cracking a joke (of course), and Jason Szelewski spouting off about some bad grade he had gotten in fourth grade. It seemed as if the boys were talking about anything that popped into their heads. Or were Mom and her film editor zipping through different interviews to get material? Madison couldn't quite figure out what was going on, and nothing seemed to make much sense.

But she kept listening.

Dan Ginsburg's voice came on.

Madison had her ear up against the door of Mom's office by now. She'd never eavesdropped like this before.

"No one in seventh grade at FHJH has a social life except with each other, you know," Dan was saying. *"But that's cool, because my friends are the best in*

the whole world, and no, I don't feel this weird pressure to ask anyone out or whatever."

Madison smiled. She'd often wondered if Dan liked *her* more than just as a friend. But he'd only said so once, and then he'd dropped it.

These days it was Lindsay who confessed to liking Dan, despite his nickname (Pork-O) and his habit of snatching food from lunch trays that were not his own. There was a lot to like about Dan, especially his freckles and his sense of humor.

Dan was still talking on the audiotape. Madison heard Mom fast-forwarding.

"If a girl liked me for real, I would probably just hang out with her the same as I do now," Dan went on on the tape. *"No biggie. I mean, nobody really dates. We're all just playing around. Um . . . you know what I mean. Some do more than others, I guess. Me, I just want someone to hang with. No biggie."*

Madison smiled again. Sometimes Dan said all the right things. She felt lucky to call him a good friend. Listening to Dan's voice through the door, Madison could understand why Lindsay had developed a little crush of her own on him. If Lindsay had been standing there right that minute, she would have been swooning over Dan's words.

The audiotape on the other side of the door clicked off.

Madison leaned forward to keep listening. What

was going on? She could hear only Mom's voice, whispers, and then a loud laugh. Who was that? Madison knew what Mom's film editor's voice sounded like and that wasn't it.

She moved her hand over the doorknob and turned it. If Madison got a peek inside, she could actually *see* who was in there—and maybe even see Dan and the other boys on their video B-reel. Would Mom let her check out the rest of the footage? She wondered what Egg or Chet or Drew had to say.

Even more important to her was to find out what Hart Jones had to say.

Madison leaned against the knob. The voices got louder. She opened the door just a crack.

The room was flooded with a bluish light from the video monitors. At one computer station, Madison recognized Frankie's back. Frankie was one of the junior techies at Budge Films. He tapped away at his keyboard, probably entering time codes. At his feet, curled up in a snug ball, Phin snored.

Dan's face took up the entire screen. He looked almost cute, Madison thought, except for an itsy-bitsy zit on his chin.

Standing nearby, Mom watched the footage. But she wasn't alone! Her hand was on someone's back. Julian Lodge!

Mom reached around Julian's waist, and he pulled her close.

Too close. What was going on?

Quickly, Madison leaped back from the doorway, shut the door, and escaped back into the brighter light of the living room.

She blinked a few times, steadying herself, unsure if she could really believe her ears . . . or her eyes.

Chapter 8

 Mom

The boycott is SO back.

I am trying really, really, REALLY hard not to jump to conclusions but it's harder than hard. After all, I KNOW WHAT I SAW. Not only did Mom a) forget to tell me about the whole filming thing at FHJH and then b) lie about it, but now she c) forgot to tell me that she was also DATING the director. Um . . . hello?! Julian Lodge? Are you kidding me?!

I could die.

This morning at breakfast, I wanted to ask Mom what was up, but it seemed better to just say nothing at all. Naturally, Mom got so mad about it that she called me Little Miss Poutypuss. I felt like I was back in nursery school when she said it. I mean, what am I supposed to respond to that?

Rude Awakening: When in doubt, pout. The right facial expression is worth a thousand words.

Oh boy. Here we go. Got to lunch early so I could write in the corner of our lunchroom table @ school but now the rest of the gang is coming and I can see

Madison snapped her laptop shut.

A long line of kids snaked through the serving area. Hart, Chet, and Dan were right at the front, trays already packed (of course). Madison tucked the computer into her orange bag. She'd sneaked in to the cafeteria before the other seventh graders, thanks to the fact that a meeting with a teacher at the end of the previous period, which was supposed to have taken twenty minutes, had only taken ten.

That meant extra time for Madison to work on her files. But now that time was being cut short.

Aimee, Fiona, and Lindsay waved from the lunchroom door. Madison needed her friends right now. There would be time enough later to finish up the Mom rant.

As Madison's BFFs grabbed trays, the boys sat down.

"Whassup, Maddie?" Chet asked as he slipped on to the bench at their orange table.

"Um . . . clouds. Or maybe hot-air balloons," Maddie said.

"You've only used that joke a hundred and one times before," Chet cracked. "You're so funny I forgot to laugh."

Madison sneered. "How can *you* forget to laugh, Chet?" Madison asked. "You're such a joke."

"Good one!" Hart said, slipping into the seat next to Madison.

Now Chet was the one sneering.

The room filled up fast. It was super noisy, with the clatter of trays and glasses that made it hard to hear.

Dan slipped into his seat near the others.

"What's up, Finnster?" Hart asked. His elbow nudged Madison's side. He smelled good today, like limes. Madison guessed he was wearing cologne.

Coolly, Madison glanced over at Hart and batted her eyelashes. Or at least she tried to bat them. Unlike her nemesis, Ivy, whenever Madison tried acting coy like that, she looked as if she had a piece of grit stuck in her eye.

"What happened to Egg?" Madison asked, attempting to change the focus of the conversation to include everyone.

"Egg's sick," Hart said.

"Yeah," Chet said. "He threw up. I thought everyone heard about it already. Imagine puking while giving an oral presentation!" Chet said.

"Gross," Madison winced.

"Luckily, Senora Diaz was in the next classroom,

94

so she took him home," Hart said. In addition to being a Spanish teacher at FHJH, Senora Diaz was Egg's mother.

"But it was not pretty," Dan said, taking a big bite of his sandwich. He chewed loudly. "At least it didn't ruin my appetite."

"Nothing ruins your appetite, man," Chet joked.

The three boys and Madison burst into laughter.

"What's so funny?" Fiona asked, walking over to the table with her lunch tray.

"Dan's doing stand-up," Hart said, slapping Dan on the back.

"We could hear you laughing like hyenas all the way across the room," Aimee added.

"Hyenas?" Chet said.

"Yeah," Fiona added. "As in, really ugly and annoying animals."

"That's too cruel," Chet gasped, pretending he'd been shot through the heart. "Even coming from you, sis."

"Like that's the worst thing you've ever been called, *bro*," Fiona moaned.

The girls all laughed. Chet and Fiona really were going at each other like angry hyenas.

"Egg went home sick," Dan finally said, filling Fiona in on the news. She looked one part disgusted and two parts concerned when she heard.

"So, does anyone get filmed later today?" Hart asked after a few quiet moments.

"Uh-huh," Lindsay nodded. "They're going to take footage at newspaper headquarters later today. I'm working on an edition of the paper. We each get to answer one question on camera."

"Did you say, 'newspaper *headquarters*'?" Chet said.

"More like the newspaper closet," Hart said.

"Oh, take a leap of imagination, you two," Lindsay said. She quickly glanced over at Maddie for support.

"Yeah, take a leap, Hart," Madison added, chuckling.

Hart laughed and nudged Madison again. "Okay, I'm leaping." He jumped away from the table and headed back toward the kitchen and the salad bar.

Madison followed him with her eyes. But as he walked away, Hart stopped by another lunchroom table.

Ivy's table.

Aimee, Fiona, and Lindsay also saw him stop there. They all stared. Ivy had reached right into the aisle as Hart walked by and literally yanked him by the arm.

Madison moaned. "This has not been the best week of my life," she said.

"What's the matter, *honey bear*?" Lindsay asked, feigning a Mom tone of voice.

"What's wrong? You mean, besides everything?" Madison asked. She took a breath. "It's this whole movie, of course. But even more than that, it's Mom—"

"You know Maddie, your mom is the best," Fiona blurted out.

All the boys nodded.

Madison cocked her head to one side. *The best*?

"Yeah, how did *you* ever get such a cool mother, Maddie?" Dan asked.

Cool?

"Yeah, I wish my mom was as cool as yours," Dan said.

"But your mom is cooler than cool," Madison said.

Dan's mother, Eileen Ginsburg, ran the office at the animal clinic in Far Hills. As far as Madison was concerned, Eileen was practically a mentor. Madison admired Eileen's collection of animal T-shirts emblazoned with funky sayings like KITTY KAT CLUB and WOOF IF YOU LOVE ME.

Madison took a large bite of her sandwich. A lettuce leaf smeared with mayonnaise fell out. Madison chewed and listened to her friends as much as she could, but secretly she kept her eyes trained on the back of Hart's head.

Hart didn't like-like Ivy, so Madison didn't really have to worry.

Did she?

They couldn't be flirting.

Could they?

In the midst of her reverie, some wild seventh

grader dropped his lunch tray. He narrowly missed impaling a passerby with a fork, and his plummeting milk carton exploded all over one of the teachers at the front of the room. The cafeteria exploded, too, into a chorus of banging and whistling for the kid. When Madison glanced over at the next table, she saw Ivy and Hart laughing together. Kids were making obnoxious comments.

"Way to drop it!"

"L-O-S-E-R!"

"Wait! Did you catch that shot?"

Madison turned. She wanted to say something, but then she spotted her mom and the crew.

"Whoa, that is so weird," Aimee blurted. "Do you think your mom knew that we were just talking about her a minute ago?"

Madison rolled her eyes. Usually, she believed in all that karmic, superstitious stuff, but not this time.

He was standing there, too.

Mom and Julian Lodge headed straight for the tables at the middle of the cafeteria. They instructed the lunch monitors on how to assist the crew in keeping the students organized. Mom carried her usual clipboard. At one point she tried making eye contact with Madison, who promptly looked away.

Julian waved his hands and prepared to make an announcement.

"Everyone, remain seated where you are, please. This is a last-minute shoot. If you did not supply a permission slip, you will need to exit the lunchroom immediately. We're just going to pan the lunchroom and do a few close-ups and establishing shots."

Right in the middle of Julian's little speech, Madison got up from of her seat at the orange table, with her tray in her hands.

"Excuse me, miss," Julian waved at Madison without quite realizing who she was. "Come back and be seated, please."

But Madison didn't listen. She gave Julian and the lunch monitor the brush-off and pushed her way through a set of doors at the side of the room.

The air in the hall smelled like glue. A teacher stood there on a stepladder, hanging objects from an art class. Madison stopped for a moment to clear her head. She'd never stormed away from anything before. Not like this. Not in front of *the entire school*.

The lunchroom doors banged open. Mom appeared.

"Maddie! What kind of a scene was that?" Mom asked. Lowering her voice to a whisper, she walked right up to Madison and took her by the arm. "What is going on with you these past few days, Maddie?"

"Nothing," Madison mumbled.

"Don't play around with me, young lady," Mom said.

Madison could tell that this scene had the potential to get ugly very fast. "You're ruining everything, Mom," she said bluntly.

Mom looked surprised. "Ruining everything?" she repeated.

Madison nodded. "Yes. Everything."

"Maddie." Mom was confused. She changed to a more playful tone, probably hoping to get Madison's spirits up again. "You and your friends are a part of something fun here. Why are you turning this into some kind of war?"

"Because it is," Madison said through clenched teeth.

Mom ran her fingers across the very top of her hair, most of which had been pulled back in a paisley scarf.

"I can't believe you're doing this to me," Mom said under her breath.

"I can't believe you're doing this to *me*," Madison said, practically spitting the words out.

By now, the lunchroom monitor had exited as well, and Madison could see kids shoving up against the cafeteria doors, hoping to get a glance of the action—her action.

Madison glanced over at them. Friends and other members of her classes stared. She'd worked so hard all week to stay away from the camera and out of the spotlight, and yet here she was, front and center of everything.

But Madison didn't care.

"Leave me alone, Mom," Madison said.

"Maddie," Mom pleaded. "Let's talk about this at

home. This is certainly not the time or the place for theatrics."

"You need to pick," Madison said.

"Pick? What?"

"Me or the camera," Madison said assertively.

"The camera? What are you talking about?" Mom was taken aback.

"Just pick, or else," Madison said.

"Or else what?" Mom asked.

At that exact moment, Julian Lodge came through the cafeteria doors, along with the film crew and the cameras.

But Mom still had not answered the question. She hadn't picked.

"Is there a problem out here? Because we need to go back inside and shoot, Francine," Julian said. He glanced at his watch. "Maddie, why don't you come back inside, too? Let's work this out."

Mom looked at Madison and then looked at Julian. Madison saw a kind of sad, faraway look in Mom's eyes. It was the same look Mom had used to get all the time during (and after) the Big D.

"Madison, we need to have a serious talk," Mom said in a low voice so no one else but they could hear.

"Yes, we do," Madison said, nodding in agreement.

But instead of turning back toward the cafeteria with Mom, Julian, and the others, Madison walked in the opposite direction, toward the lockers.

And Mom didn't follow.

Chapter 9

Other than those times when Mom had been away traveling or when Madison had gone on sleepovers, Friday night was the first time ever that Madison had not given Mom a kiss good night.

Of course, no kiss meant that Madison had gone to bed angry. And after going to bed angry, all Madison could do was toss and turn all night long. So by the time Saturday morning came around, an exhausted Madison could barely crawl out from under the covers. This morning, she was too tired even to sit at her desk, so Madison dragged her laptop on to the bed. At around ten-thirty, Madison Insta-Messaged her keypal, hoping to catch Bigwheels online even though she knew it was early in Washington State, where Bigwheels lived.

In fact, Bigwheels *was* online.

\<MadFinn\>: OMG I need u
\<Bigwheels\>: Helloooooo well I'm
here
\<MadFinn\>: is it only 8 or
something where u r?
\<Bigwheels\>: I woke up early b/c my
Dad is running a marathon 2day
even tho it's so cold here
\<MadFinn\>: That's 2C4W
\<Bigwheels\>: so WTBD?
\<MadFinn\>: HUGE fight w/Mom
\<Bigwheels\>: ONO what about?
\<MadFinn\>: this school video
\<Bigwheels\>: &?
\<MadFinn\>: I hate her well no I
hate IT
\<Bigwheels\>: Y???
\<MadFinn\>: 8>} im scared of making
a fool of me
\<Bigwheels\>: u know my new class
pal told me 2day to not be afraid
of stuff and I think u should try
that 2
\<MadFinn\>: huh? Y did yr class pal
say that?
\<Bigwheels\>: I was chicken about
something a song I had to sing in
chorus
\<MadFinn\>: U didn't tell me that
\<Bigwheels\>: yeah Pinkie is soooo
nice

<MadFinn>: does she have a real name?
<Bigwheels>: yeah it's Melody & we
    talked in school every day this
    week

Madison leaned back into her pillows for a second. How did Bigwheels's class pal find her way into their online chat *again*? Weren't they just talking about Madison and *her* problems with Mom? What was Melody doing in the mix?

<Bigwheels>: maddie???

Madison didn't know what to say. Normally, Bigwheels would just know all the right things to say when Madison was having a hard time. But for some reason today was different. Bigwheels was only *half* there.

Phinnie jumped on top of the covers on Madison's bed, nearly knocking the laptop off the side. Madison grabbed it in the nick of time. She glanced back at the screen.

<Bigwheels>: Hello yo? R U THERE??
    DRA . . .
<MadFinn>: i'm here i'm here
<Bigwheels>: whats wrong?
<MadFinn>: I told u
<Bigwheels>: that isn't all, I can
    tell

```
<MadFinn>: well the truth is that I
    saw mom with this guy who happens
    to be the guy directing the movie
    at our school
<Bigwheels>: what were they doing?
<MadFinn>: Standing 2 close
<Bigwheels>: Whoa
<MadFinn>: I know it bummed me out
<Bigwheels>: Y?
```

Madison sat there for a moment and thought about Bigwheels's question

Why?

Why did it bother her to find Mom and Julian together like that?

Phin's ears perked up the way they always did when he heard a funny noise. He jumped back down off the bed and started scratching at Madison's bedroom door.

"Maddie?"

Mom knocked softly from the other side of the door, but her voice was clear.

"Maddie? I know you don't feel well, but you just got a call from Dan. He's down at the clinic, and he wanted to know if you're still coming in today."

Madison gasped. It was Saturday. She'd completely forgotten. "Uh . . . I . . ." Madison stammered. She didn't want to break the boycott again, but she had to talk to Mom now. "Is Dan still on the phone? Um . . ."

She heard Mom try to turn the doorknob, but it was locked.

"Maddie, please open this door right now. You know what I've said about locked doors in this house. I don't want to have to ask you again. . . ."

Mom started in on one of her lectures. Madison glanced quickly back down at the laptop screen.

```
<MadFinn>: OMG I have 2 go
<Bigwheels>: wait but u didn't
    finish
<MadFinn>: I fogot somthg imptant I
    hve 2 go NOW
```

Madison signed off without spelling anything correctly—and without a proper good-bye to her keypal. She shut the laptop and raced over to the locked door. With a click, she turned the knob.

". . . And I don't think that you're even listening to me when I tell you . . ."

Mom stood back, eyes wide open.

"There, that's better," she said, stopping her lecture. "Now, what's this about going to the clinic today? You didn't mention anything to me."

"I forgot, Mom. Really, it's not a big deal," Madison said.

"Well, I think you should know—" Mom started to say.

Madison cut her off. "Look, I can't stand around talking now," she said, tearing through her closet. "I need to get dressed really fast and get over there."

"Madison, there's something important you should—"

"How about these? Do you like these? Oh, how about these?"

Madison yanked on a pair of jeans, even though they were paint-stained. She figured that grubby was better if she was going to be handling new puppies and the puppy chow and poop that went along with the job.

"How are you planning to get to the animal clinic?" Mom asked.

"Bus," Madison said. But she quickly added, "Unless . . ."

"Unless I give you a ride?" Mom said, raising her eyebrows.

Madison nodded, trying to smile. She felt bad asking Mom to drive her to the clinic after everything that had happened. But at the same time, she needed to get there pronto. A ride in the car was the fastest option.

Mom didn't say much on the way over. That was because Madison wouldn't let her talk. Every time Mom started to say something, Madison cut her off. They hit all green lights on the way over, so it was only seven minutes from the time of Dan's call until the moment they pulled up in front of the clinic.

"So, here we are," Mom announced, gripping the steering wheel.

Madison scanned the street. She saw the large bus with the sign that read: MR. MOTION PICTURES, parked next to the clinic.

"What's *that* doing here?" Madison asked.

Mom exhaled deeply. "I tried telling you," she said.

"What? You didn't tell me anything," Mom said.

Mom looked Madison square in the eye. "Madison, you barely let me say anything to you these days. I give up."

"Mom," Madison said meekly. She looked back out of the window. "Why is the film crew here?"

"I set it up with Dan's mother, Eileen. I heard about the new puppies from her, and Julian thought it would be a great place to show student volunteerism."

"But Mom, this is *my* special place," Madison said.

"Other kids volunteer here, too. And Eileen and Dan were thrilled about the idea."

Madison didn't know what to say to that. She swallowed her feelings and opened the car door.

"Are you coming, then?" Madison asked Mom. She assumed, of course, that Mom would be involved in the shoot that day.

"No." Mom shook her head. "Julian is probably inside," she added.

"I know. Why aren't you with him?" Madison asked. "You guys were together yesterday. Aren't you always together?"

"What?" Mom said, looking confused. "What does that have to do with anything?"

"Ha."

"What's 'ha' supposed to mean?" Mom asked.

"You know," Madison said, making one of her sour faces. Then she said a polite enough good-bye, but slammed the door.

"Just call me when you need a ride back home," Mom yelled through the car window.

"Fine," Madison said, without turning around.

Madison knew that if she'd had eyes in the back of her head she would have seen Mom waving and blowing a kiss. One of Mom's biggest rules was never to go to bed angry or part ways with someone angry. But in one short day, Madison had done both of those things.

As soon as Madison stepped inside the warm clinic, however, her spirits improved. Something about that place always made her happy, no matter what.

Eileen sat at the front desk, petting a gray Siamese cat.

"Madison's here!" Eileen cried. "Dan's been waiting for you, dearie," she said. "They all have."

Madison hung down her head. "I know. Sorry."

Dan raced into the front waiting room from the back of the clinic. He had on a white apron. He'd been cleaning out cages and feeding some of the sick animals inside.

"Where were you?" Dan asked Madison. He

lowered his voice. "I almost flipped out when you didn't show up at ten. Not because of the puppies, though. You won't believe what happened here this morning. My mom didn't tell me. . . ."

"I know, I know," Madison interrupted. "The film crew is here."

"You know?" Dan smacked the side of his forehead. "Crazy, huh? But kind of cool, too, you know?"

"Not to me," Madison said. "Dan, you know I've been doing everything in my power *not* to get on film."

"But this is different. This is about the puppies," Dan said with a grin.

Madison couldn't help grinning back at him.

"Come and see them," Dan said, inviting her into the back room by the animal cages.

In one corner, Madison spotted the mommy dog. By her belly were the squirmy pups. There were three light brown ones and four with little spots. One had a black spot on its back that looked a little like a bull's-eye.

Madison leaned down near the pups and took a deep breath. They were beautiful. The cage smelled like wet dog, but Madison didn't mind. Their eyes were barely open; paws were curled out trying to make contact with the mommy dog's belly. The mother looked totally wiped out.

"How cool is this?" Dan asked. He lightly put his

arm around Madison's shoulder and pointed to one of the pups that had whitish fur. "I already named that one. He's the runt of the litter, but I think he's going to grow up to be the best puppy of them all. I call him Frosty."

Madison wondered if maybe Dan had dreamed up the name Frosty because of Lindsay, since her last name was Frost. Maybe he was in the process of crushing on Lindsay, too? Or was that just wishful thinking?

Flash! Zzzzzzt!

Madison turned around to find the bright light of a video camera focused on her and Dan. She could just barely make out a face beyond the glare.

"Julian?"

"Okay, we got that shot. Fantastic," Julian said. He stood back, hands in his pockets. "What a pleasant surprise," he said to Madison. "I didn't know you were a volunteer here."

Madison did a double take. "You didn't know? Wait a minute. I thought Mom told you everything. I mean, you guys are close. . . . Right?"

"Close?" Julian cleared his throat and then said Mom's name warmly. "Honestly, Francine never mentioned that you were a volunteer, Madison, which is funny, because she knew I was coming here to film today."

Madison put her hands on her hips. "So, your being here at the place where I just happen to

volunteer is a total coincidence?" she asked skepti-
cally.

"It appears so," Julian said. "Now, for our next
shot, I'd like to . . ."

Madison tuned out as Julian continued talking.
He was going on about where to stand and what
animals he wanted to get in the shot. Madison was
speechless. He *had* to be lying.

"What's that all about?" Dan whispered in her
ear.

"Hmmm?" Madison mumbled. Her head whirred.
Coincidence? Impossible!

Puppies crawled and stretched over each other to
get to the mommy dog's belly. One little one got
pushed out of the way, so Madison placed it back in
the thick of the action, where it found a place to
suckle.

Eileen came up behind Madison. "You can take
one home if you want," she said.

Madison turned around. "Me?" she asked. "No, I
can't."

"Why not?" Julian asked aloud. He'd overheard
the exchange. "Your pug would love to have a play-
mate, I'm sure."

Madison didn't like the fact that Julian knew
about her dog—or anything else personal about her,
for that matter.

"I don't think Phin would like another dog
around the house," Madison said bluntly.

Dan tapped her on the shoulder. "Excuse me, Maddie, but we have some more work to do. Can you come into the back and help me clean out the operating room? Dr. Wing will be back in an hour or so, and he has another surgery this afternoon."

"Surgery? Well, volunteers have a lot of responsibility here, don't they?" Julian commented.

Madison smiled politely. "I guess so," she said. "Dan knows more than me . . ."

"Yeah," Dan said. "It gets real busy, especially around the holidays."

"Why is that?" Julian asked, curious.

"People give other people pets for Christmas and Hanukkah and stuff," Dan said.

"And it's really sad," Madison said.

"Sad? Why?" Julian asked.

"It's not sad . . . it's *mean*!" Dan said. "Here's what happens. People buy these pets, but then they decide they can't take care of the animal, so it comes here to be adopted by a new family. Can you imagine getting a little puppy and then giving him back?"

"I hadn't thought about it before now," Julian said. "Know what? You kids have inspired me."

"Inspired?" Madison said.

"Indeed," Julian said. "I think that I want to explore this more in our film. I want to understand junior-high-school kids who are really out helping the community. Kids like you."

"Like us? Gee," Madison said. She was speechless again, but this time it was for a good reason.

"I'm very impressed by you both," Julian said, grinning.

"No doubt," Dan said.

From that moment on, Madison couldn't wipe the smile off her face. And by the time Mom came by with the car to pick her up, Madison had to admit that she was actually starting to *like* Julian.

But just a teeny bit.

Chapter 10

Fiona's mother, Mrs. Waters, stood over the sink rinsing her hands. She turned and dropped spoonfuls of brown batter on to a wide cookie sheet.

"Second batch coming right up!" she announced to everyone as she shoved the sheet into the oven.

Fiona, Madison, Aimee, Lindsay, Chet, Drew, Hart, and Dan stood around the island in the middle of the kitchen, drooling. Mrs. Waters made the best chocolate-chunk cookies in the universe. Since the group had munched its way through an entire batch in less than a half hour, Mrs. Waters agreed to make another batch.

"Thanks, Mom," Fiona said, grabbing the bowl that had held batter to wash it out.

The weather looked dreary that Sunday, so Fiona and Chet had invited everyone over at the last minute. Madison—and everyone else, for that matter—jumped at the chance to hang out together. Usually when the crew was all together like this, it meant a lot of laughs. Today especially, it took Madison's mind off her problems. This week Madison wanted to take a break from the film and Julian and everything else that had been bugging her.

Egg wasn't there. He was home, nursing a bug of his own. Somehow he'd caught a stomach virus. He couldn't eat. He couldn't even drink a glass of water. Fiona had text-messaged him earlier in the day asking him join the midafternoon party, but he had declined. He said he was permanently attached to his parents' couch.

"At least Egg wasn't sick for the film shoot," Chet said.

"I hope he'll be back in school Monday," Fiona said. She always worried about him.

"Speaking of the film shoot, did you guys see Ivy on Friday?" Drew asked the group. "I always knew she was a show-off, but this was ridiculous."

"What happened?" Madison asked, curious.

"I heard she went into her individual interview on Thursday and she talked for, like, twenty minutes more than anyone else," Drew said. "But then she asked Julian if she could answer some more questions on Friday, too."

"Figures," Aimee said. "She always has to do everything better than everyone else."

Lindsay nodded. "I only talked for ten minutes, tops. What could she possibly have said?"

"Who cares?" Chet said.

Fiona chuckled. "Finally, we agree on something." She gave him a high five. No one wanted to talk about the enemy or the drones.

Although they all went back to the subject of the cookies baking in the oven, Madison couldn't stop thinking about Ivy.

What *could* Ivy possibly have talked about for so long?

"Okay, guys," Hart said. "No offense but I'm getting bored."

"Me, too," Lindsay admitted.

"So what else can we do?" Fiona asked.

Chet said they should head outside for a game of touch football, but then everyone decided it was just too cold.

"Let's just play a game," Drew suggested.

"Yes!" Chet said. "Spin the bottle."

"Yeah, right," Aimee cracked.

"How about a board game?" Madison said.

No one seemed very enthusiastic about the idea of Risk or Monopoly or Cranium or even cards.

"Okay. What about Truth or Dare?" Fiona asked aloud.

Madison made a face. "With the guys?" she asked.

"Yeah, great idea!" Chet said with a glint in his eye. "I get to make up a dare for Fiona."

"You wish," Fiona said.

"No way am I playing Truth or Dare," Aimee said. "I am not sharing any truths with Chet or any of you boys."

Madison laughed. She imagined what it would be like to play a tense game of Truth or Dare with this crowd. What if the truth came out about how much Aimee *really* liked Ben Buckley? Or worse— what if the truth came out about how much Madison *really* liked Hart Jones? Even though Madison's crush was now common knowledge, she didn't want to have to answer any specific (and embarrassing) questions about it.

"I'm with Aim," Madison said. "No Truth or Dare."

"I know what game we can play," Hart said. "Assassin."

"Great idea!" Fiona exclaimed. "Okay. So, who's the assassin?"

"Duh, Fiona," Chet growled. "You don't say who the assassin is yet—that's the whole point of the game."

Fiona rolled her eyes. "I hope *you're* not," she said.

Having decided upon a group activity they could all agree upon, the kids shuffled in to the living room to begin playing. The eight of them formed a tight circle. The aroma of fresh-baked chocolate-chunk cookies filled the living room.

Madison sat cross-legged on the floor next to Hart, trying hard not to stare at the side of his head. Every time he leaned back, he touched her arm—just a little, but he made definite contact, and she liked it. Madison kept trying to find new and inconspicuous reasons to adjust her position so that she could bump into him as much as possible.

Drew sat on the left side of Madison, with Aimee on his left. Across from Madison, Fiona sat cross-legged in a big chair. Next to her, Chet sat in a director's chair he'd pulled in from his Dad's office.

For some reason, Dan and Lindsay ended up squished together on the love seat. Was it karma? Madison could tell that Lindsay was feeling a little bit self-conscious about that seating arrangement. She had her arms crossed in front of her the way she always did when she was nervous. Any minute now, Madison expected her to start talking non-stop. Lindsay could never shut up when she was nervous.

Chet held a pad of paper, a pen, and his tattered red baseball cap. He carefully tore off eight scraps of paper and scribbled circles on each one. In the center of one circle, he placed a single black X.

"So, we each pick these out of this hat," Chet said. "And whoever gets the X has to be the assassin."

"This is so cool!" Lindsay said. "I haven't played this in forever."

"Me, neither," said Dan.

"I remember playing this at camp once," Lindsay said without taking a single breath. "And this kid who was the assassin actually forgot he was the assassin, and so we kept playing, but no one was dying, and then finally someone said, 'What's going on?' and so we had to start all over again, and it was funny because . . ."

Chet made a face as if to say, "Who is this crazy person?" Madison wanted to laugh. Lindsay was off and running, or rather, off and talking. But Dan didn't look bothered one bit by Lindsay's talk. He listened attentively.

Madison glanced over at Fiona and mouthed the words *How sweet is that?*

With a flourish, Chet placed the scraps into a hat and shook it dramatically.

"Ta-da!" he announced. "Okay, Fiona. Pick first."

Fiona grabbed her scrap. She made a funny face. "Aha!" she declared.

"Wait!" Chet barked. "Don't give anything away."

"Hey, moron," Fiona barked back, "I'm just play-ing the game. Relax."

Everyone else took their scraps, too, and stared at them.

Madison's scrap didn't have an *X*. She crushed the paper in her palm, however, and tried to act as if maybe—just maybe—she were the real assassin. As she scanned the circle for the true assassin, Madison tried not to make eye contact with any of her friends for too long. The whole point was not to get winked at immediately.

After five minutes, however, three people were out of the game: Fiona, Lindsay, and Aimee. Fiona went into the kitchen to check on the cookies. Aimee crawled over behind Madison. Lindsay simply sat back on the sofa, grinning and (Madison noticed) staring at Dan.

Madison was the only girl remaining. There was no one left to give a clue to the true assassin's identity. Madison was on her own.

By that point, the room had dissolved into silence. Madison glanced quickly at Hart and then Chet.

Drew made a joke and fell backward. "I am so dead," he said, getting back up to join the others.

"Maddie, are you the assassin?" Hart asked. He stared at Madison for a second and then glanced over at Dan.

All at once, Dan tumbled on to the sofa—right on top of Lindsay.

"Oh," Dan said, scrambling to sit back up again. "I'm so sorry."

By now, Lindsay had turned four shades of purple. Madison had never seen her blush like that before.

That was when Madison turned back to the circle

and pointed a finger at Chet. "You want everyone to think you're the assassin!" Madison said. "But the assassin is . . . YOU!" Madison turned to Hart.

Everyone laughed out loud, including him.

"You got me, Finnster. I thought for sure I could trick you."

"Snack time!" Fiona cried as she walked back into the room carrying a basket of the just-baked chocolate-chunk cookies. The basket was steaming.

The boys leaped from where they sat to grab fist-fuls of the cookies.

Dan got there first. He always got to the sweets and snacks before everyone else. But then he did something surprising.

He took one cookie and handed it to Lindsay.

"For you," Dan said softly.

"Oh, boy," Madison thought. Dan was actually giving up a freshly baked chocolate-chunk cookie for Lindsay?

Although almost everyone in the game had been assassinated, Dan was the true goner.

Madison came home from Fiona's to find Mom still busy working in her office. Mom sat in practically the same spot where she had been sitting when Madison had left earlier that day.

"Hey," Madison mumbled as she smoothly slid past the office.

"Huh? Maddie?"

Mom barely had enough time to poke her head out from behind the computer—let alone say anything in response.

"Oh, Maddie! I'm so glad you're home, because I need to—"

Madison didn't hear the end of the sentence. She was already upstairs in her room, booting up her laptop. She opened a new file.

 Games

Rude Awakening: It's not how you play the game. It's whether you win or lose.

I'm the Assassin champ today. But how do I win the game I'm playing with Mom?

It's so hard not to obsess about this stuff that's going on with Mom and the school video and Julian Lodge. My head is spinning, spinning. I've been thinking about it nonstop. Why did the film crew have to come to OUR school? The worst part is that I can't talk to Mom about her job without her getting upset and defensive and weird. I can't ask her personal questions either, like whether she's seeing Mr. Bigshot Film Guy Julian. I mean, I can always talk to Dad about things like that. Why is Mom so hard to get through to?

"Maddie, why didn't you stop in my office to say

hi?" Mom said, appearing at the doorway to Madison's bedroom.

"Mom!" Madison cried, nearly falling backward off her chair. "How long have you been standing there?"

"I just walked up. What's going on? You just walk in the door and sweep past my office like that?" Mom asked.

Madison shrugged. "Yeah. I guess."

"Well, I'm glad you're back," Mom continued. "How was your day?"

"Fine."

"Were all your friends there?" Mom asked.

Madison nodded. "Mom, we need to talk."

Mom nodded. "Mmmm. We do."

"Yeah," Madison said, mustering her courage. She needed to tell Mom what was really on her mind.

"Oh, Maddie, I'd love to talk. But right this moment I need to dash out of here just to run an errand. Would you be okay here by yourself for an hour or so?" Mom asked.

"Yeah, of course," Madison said, sounding disappointed.

"Honey bear, I promise to be back in a flash," Mom said, turning away. "How about I grab some Chinese or pizza on the way home? We can talk over dinner."

"Takeout?" Madison said to herself. "Great."

"Great!"

124

Madison heard Mom rustling through her papers downstairs. Then the door slammed.

Madison stood up from her desk and closed the laptop. Phin danced around her feet as she walked across the room.

"Why does Mom never find time to talk?" Madison asked him.

"Rooooowwwwf!" Phin growled.

"It makes me mad, too," Madison barked back.

Together they trotted down the stairs and into the kitchen.

Madison pulled open the refrigerator door and grabbed a can of root beer that had been on ice for a while. Really cold root beer always tasted so good.

The door to Mom's office was wide open. From where she stood, Madison saw piles of papers and videocassettes. She carried the can of soda into the office, collapsed into Mom's whirly Aeron office chair, and spun around.

What had Mom been so busy working on?

The computer hummed steadily. A freeze-frame of the exterior of the school glowed from the screen. Along the bottom, Madison read the words JUNIOR HIGH ISN'T ALWAYS EASY.

Madison had to laugh. She leaned in toward the computer keyboard. She remembered Mom's rule about never touching anything, especially when Mom was in the middle of a project. (One time, she'd sneaked into Mom's office and almost deleted an entire set of files.) But her fingers grazed the keys even so.

The screen went blank. A menu appeared, asking Madison if she wanted to share, save, pause, or continue.

Madison quickly weighed her options. She examined the label on the videotape that was currently sticking out of the player. It read: SCHOOL EXTERIOR. Madison glanced at the dozens of other videos on the desk and floor.

Share or save? Pause or continue?

Out of the corner of one eye, Madison saw another video label with a name she recognized: DALY—DUNMORE, 7.

Madison snatched that tape and shoved it into the machine. Was this Daly the same Daly as *Poison Ivy* Daly?

The tracking on the video took a minute or two to adjust; but then a familiar face appeared.

"Take four," a voice said before clapping down a marker that showed how much footage had been shot to date.

This was the right Daly. Poison Ivy sat there, facing the camera, her red hair looking a lot frizzier than usual.

Madison turned up the volume. It looked as though Ivy's lips were moving faster than the sound was coming out; but Madison could hear every word perfectly. Ivy talked nonstop about everything, from boys to science to love/hate relationships with teachers.

And then she did something extraordinary.

Ivy began talking about *Madison*.

Chapter 11

 Ivy on Video

Rude Awakening: Sometimes the truth hurts but most of the time it just FREAKS ME OUT.

I've said this a million times, but sometimes Ivy is like Dr. Jekyll and Mr. Hyde the way she says the meanest, most obnoxious things and then all of a sudden she comes right out and says something NICE.

On the video B-reel that I was watching, Ivy got asked all these quasi-personal questions about school and life. She actually said that the only thing she really regrets about being in junior high is losing some of the friends and memories she had from elementary school. And then she named me. Me? ME! Whoa.

Well, she didn't actually use my name, but I just know it was me she was talking about. She said something like, "I used to be friends with this girl in my class but things have gotten really ugly in junior high and we're so different now and we hardly speak and sometimes I wonder what it would be like if we hadn't stopped being friends."

I had to replay the question and answer just to make sure I wasn't hearing things. Not only did Ivy say what she said, but at the end she confessed that she thought maybe we'd be friends again one day. LOL. As if!

I know the real deal. She probably just wants to come across as sympathetic so she can kiss up to Julian for whatever reason and become the star of this dumb movie even though it's not a real movie. ARGH! This whole scene has just gotten so out of

Knock, knock. Rattle, rattle.
Madison's head shot up. The doorknob clicked again. Madison had locked the door so no one could come inside.

"Madison, are you in there?"

It was Mom—and her voice sounded pretty tense. Madison was feeling a little tense, too, after everything she'd seen on the video. She gnawed on a fingernail.

"Mom?" Madison said.

"Maddie, open this door, now. I mean it. I told you earlier this week . . ."

"Yes, yes, I know. Don't lock it. I'm opening it right now," Madison said.

She turned the knob.

Mom gave her a stern look. "Where have you been while I was out?"

"Um . . ." Madison shrugged. "Here. There. Everywhere."

"Like, my office?"

"Oh. Yeah. But just for a minute," Madison said. "I went in to borrow a . . . piece of . . . um . . . a paper clip."

"A paper clip?" Mom said. "Maddie, don't lie to me. Please."

"I wouldn't . . . um . . . lie," Madison said, crossing her fingers and toes at the exact same time.

"I don't even have any paper clips," Mom said.

"I didn't know that," Madison said.

"Madison, I trust you when I go out," Mom said. "And I don't understand why you feel the need to deceive me when I ask you a very simple question."

"Mom, I just said I don't—and I didn't—lie."

Mom raised her eyebrows and held up a cassette. "Then would you mind telling me how the copy of this Daly-Dunmore video was inserted into the video player in my office? I wasn't watching this when I left."

130

Madison gulped and started chewing on the same finger. "You weren't?"

"Look, Maddie, is there something you need to tell me?" Mom asked.

"Er . . . no," Madison said quietly. "I don't think so."

"Maybe something like 'I'm sorry I was poking around your office materials, Mom'?" Mom said. "I leave you for two minutes and you ransack my entire room?"

"Ransack?" Madison asked with disbelief. "I only sat in one chair. . . ."

"Is that so?"

"I didn't touch much, I swear. . . ."

"I don't know what to think anymore, Maddie," Mom said, shaking her head. "You certainly are keeping your share of secrets these days, young lady."

Madison bristled. She understood why Mom was upset.

But Madison was upset, too.

"Secrets? What are you talking about?" Madison sniped. "What about *your* secrets?"

"*My* secrets?" Mom cried.

"Yeah," Madison said.

She and Mom stood toe to toe, eye to eye.

"I don't have any secrets," Mom said firmly.

"You don't?" Madison bit her lip. "What about Julian Lodge?"

"What about him?"

"I saw you."

131

"Saw what?" Mom chuckled.

"He had his hand on your back. . . ."

"Madison! Don't be ridiculous. When did you see this?" Mom's eyes darted from side to side.

"See? Now you're lying to me. This is so totally unfair."

"Unfair? Oh, Maddie, don't you think you're being a little dramatic?"

"You always say that!" Madison whined. "How can you be mad at me for lying when you won't tell me the truth about Julian? I saw you, Mom. I saw you holding each other. Right here in our house. And I wasn't spying on you, if that's what you're thinking. I just walked into your office and saw you there right out in the open."

"Oh, Madison," Mom said quietly. "I didn't want you to find out like this. I was going to tell you. When the time was right . . ."

When the time was right?

Madison's stomach did a major flip-flop. Her worst suspicions were confirmed.

"You see," Mom continued. "I've known Julian for years. He and I have crossed paths on various film projects. And this time around, well . . . we just hit it off. We have a lot in common. So . . ."

Madison's face fell. "So he's your boyfriend?"

"No," Mom said quickly. "Nothing that serious. Not yet."

"Not yet?"

Madison felt the tears welling up inside.

"You told me once, Mom, that if you ever dated anyone you would tell me first; you would tell me everything," Madison said. "But you told me nothing about Julian, even after I met him."

"I wanted to tell you," Mom said. "But once we started filming at Far Hills, I thought it would be better to wait. At least until we stopped working on the project at your school."

"How could you lie to me, Mom?" Madison said, her voice cracking a little bit.

The phone rang, but they both stood there, not moving. Somewhere downstairs, the answering machine clicked on.

"Hello, Maddie? Are you there? It's Daddy, honey. I just got stuck in traffic downtown—oh, hey, it's moving again. I'll be right there."

The phone machine clicked off. Neither Madison nor Mom had moved a single inch, although both of them heard Dad's message clearly.

"Dad," Madison said simply. She clutched at her middle, woozy. "Does Dad know about your new boyfriend?"

Mom shook her head. "No. No."

Madison took a deep breath. "Does anyone else know?" she asked.

Mom nodded. "Well, Olga next door knows. She always knows everything that goes on around here. And some of my coworkers know, of course. It's too hard to keep these things private when we're working late nights. I think I mentioned something to Aimee's mother, too. . . ."

"Mrs. Gillespie? And all those other people?" Madison cried. "But you didn't tell me? I can't believe you."

"Maddie, I'm very sorry if you feel hurt," Mom said. "But I think maybe all of this is just a misunderstanding."

Madison blinked so she wouldn't show Mom her tears. She rubbed her left eye and shook her head in utter disbelief.

"Look, I don't want to fight," Mom said.

"I don't want to fight, either," Madison said defensively.

Ding-a-ding. Ding-a-ding.

The doorbell was losing its ring. It sounded more like a low wail than a proper ring; but the sound suited the moment.

Someone *was* downstairs.

"Cavalry here!" Dad cried from below. "Where's my girl?"

The moment Phinnie heard Dad's voice, he leaped off Madison's bed, where he'd been nestling among the pillows. He scooted downstairs, and Madison knew that within minutes he'd be attacking Dad with wet, doggy kisses.

Mom just stood there, rubbing her hands together. She shook her head sadly. "I don't know what else to say about this, honey bear," Mom said. "I don't want you to be upset because I'm seeing someone . . . and I certainly don't want you to leave the house tonight being angry."

Madison looked away. "But I am angry," she grunted.

"Maddie, don't be this way," Mom said.

"Be what way, Mom? I'm not the one who started seeing someone and kept it a big, fat secret."

"Oh, Madison, can we please take the drama down a notch? I said I was sorry. And I am."

Madison picked up her woolly cardigan sweater and gently pushed past Mom. She took the stairs two at a time and headed for the front door.

"Madison? Come back here. Please."

But Madison didn't turn back. She thought for sure Mom would follow her downstairs, but she didn't. Dad waited by the front door.

"Hey, Dad," Madison said, giving him a peck on the cheek. She grabbed a nubby hat and gray scarf and her warm pink peacoat and then kissed Phin.

She and Dad walked out the door, leaving the dog inside.

"Why so glum, chum?" Dad asked as they walked down the driveway to his car. "Seriously, Maddie, are you okay? Where's your mother?"

"She's upstairs," Madison grunted. "And the answer to your question is, no, Dad, I'm not okay. I'm worse than glum."

A quizzical look spread across Dad's face. He blew on his hands for warmth and opened the car door for Madison. Then he walked around and slipped into the driver's seat. Madison attached her seat belt.

The interior of his car smelled hot, stuffy, like popcorn.

"Are you planning on telling me what's up?" Dad asked before putting the car into gear.

"No," Madison said. She didn't want to say anything more. She just wanted to go.

The ride over to Dad's apartment took longer than usual. The traffic was just as bad as what Dad had hit on the way over. Two cars had slid into a barrier, knocking over a pole that landed across the icy road.

Dad zigzagged onto a crooked side street to avoid the jam.

"Let's take back roads so we don't sit for a half hour," Dad said to Madison. "And while we ride, you're going to tell me the truth about what's going on. The truth, Maddie."

Madison wasn't a hundred percent sure what the truth was anymore. Some of the things she'd believed were true about Mom had turned out to be outright lies. So she kept her mouth shut. Besides, she didn't want to start talking and then spill the beans about Julian Lodge.

Thankfully, Dad didn't push his interrogation. By

the time they arrived at his apartment, he had resorted to his usual tactic: telling bad jokes to break the tension.

Madison's stepmother, Stephanie, was sprawled on the couch at the apartment when they arrived. She was just tying up the stitches on a few patches from an old crazy quilt she'd purchased at an antiques fair.

"Hello, you two," Stephanie said as Dad and Madison walked inside.

Madison kissed her hello.

"I have some unfortunate news," Stephanie said.

"Oh, no," Dad moaned. "Break it to us gently."

"I burned the soufflé."

"Burned? No!" Dad said incredulously. "How could you? I left it on a low setting, didn't I?"

The three of them went into the kitchen to examine the soufflé in question. It didn't even look very crispy, Madison thought to herself. Dad was usually such a perfectionist when it came to cooking dinner.

"Well . . . I don't have enough eggs to make another one," Dad said. "We'll have to make do."

"I don't care if it's burned, Dad," Madison said, trying to be nice. "I'll eat some anyway. I bet it still tastes good. Everything you cook tastes good."

Dad gave Madison an affectionate pinch. "That's my honey," he said. "I guess I can scrape off the edges that are burnt, too. We'll live."

"I took my eye off the clock, and I'm really sorry, Jeff," Stephanie said. "I know you wanted this to be a special dinner."

"Nah, forget it. Nothing to be sorry about," Dad said, kissing Stephanie hard on the lips. They always seemed to embrace each other warmly like that. Sometimes it made Madison feel slightly uncomfortable, but other times—like now—it made her feel like a witness to real love and understanding.

"There's always a little burn around the edges of life anyhow," Dad said, winking at Madison.

Madison smiled. She knew what he was talking about. Even though Dad didn't know the exact details, he knew that there were some serious burned edges on Madison and Mom's relationship, too, right now.

Sometimes dads could be so smart.

After dinner, before heading home, Madison dashed into Dad's study and quickly got online to check her e-mailbox. Checking bigfishbowl.com always helped lift her spirits. She could surf over to the Ask the Blowfish section or read some of the funny postings on the main bulletin board. Or she could just check her own mailbox. Tonight, Madison was hoping for e-mail from Bigwheels.

The e-mail was there!

But it wasn't exactly the kind of e-mail Madison had hoped for.

From: Bigwheels
To: MadFinn
Subject: How R UUUUU?
Date: Sun 30 Jan 7:26 PM

I'm sooo sorry but this has been a
nutty wk. we've been doing these
joint Web pages w/our class pals.
Melody & I made a page with
pictures from Washington and
Australia. It's VVC. But u know
that. I have 2 send u the link if
we actually post it. I have never
had sooo much fun in a school
assignment as I have w/my class
pal. U should get one, too. It
changed the whole way I use the
Internet.

Meanwhile, in other news, I'm
getting a B- for that reading class
I told u about. I thought I would
get at least an A- but I'm not.
That's such a tough teacher. Melody
says that she actually got a lower
grade on her last English assignment
in Australia, too. Isn't that a
cool coincidence? We really do have
plenty in common.

BTW what's the latest with Hart
and school? Are they done w/that

movie and can I see it? U haven't told me enuf. WBSTS. That means now.

Yours till the class pals,

Vicki (aka Bigwheels)

Madison reread the message. She wanted to respond. She wanted to tell Bigwheels that she was super sorry about the missed A-. She also wanted to answer questions and pass along the latest scoop on Hart.

Madison clicked REPLY.

But then she hit DELETE.

Then REPLY.

DELETE.

She was giving herself an indecision headache.

Finally, Madison clicked the POWER button, and the laptop went off. After all, what was the point of sending a message? Bigwheels had Melody to tell her all those things now, didn't she? She'd even signed it "Yours till the class pals."

"You ready to go, hon?" Stephanie asked from the doorway to Dad's office. "Your dad just went down to get the car out of the garage."

Madison nodded. She logged off Dad's computer. "Thanks for dinner," she told Stephanie.

Stephanie grabbed her by the shoulders and

leaned in for a big hug. "You seem a little down. You okay?" Stephanie asked.

"Yeah, well . . . it's just a Mom thing . . ." Madison mumbled. "And my keypal is being weird."

"Oh, I see," Stephanie said. "Well, I'm sure you'll work things out. You always do."

Madison shrugged. "I guess," she said, linking arms with Stephanie.

She wanted to believe that that was true.

But deep down, she wasn't so sure.

Chapter 12

"What did I miss?" Egg asked Madison in homeroom on Monday morning.

Madison rolled her eyes at him. "Everything," she muttered.

Although Egg had happily recovered from his stomach bug, he was disappointed to learn that he'd missed some of the filming—as well as the cool game of Assassin at Fiona's.

A few desks away, Poison Ivy primped and posed in a handheld mirror.

"You know, the filming is over," Madison whispered.

Ivy shot her a look. "I know that," she said. "But you never know when you need to look good. I mean, duh. You know *that*, Madison . . . well, er . . .

maybe you don't. It's not like you're jumping off the pages of *Cosmo* or anything."

"Excuse me?" Madison said, surprised. After all, this was the same Ivy who had told the video camera that she wished Madison had never stopped being her friend.

What a poser.

When Madison tried to make eye contact with Ivy, the enemy whipped out her cell phone and punched a few keys. Madison figured Ivy was probably text-messaging one of the drones, as usual.

Why was she way more interested in berry gloss and her glittery cell phone cover than she was in Madison? Was everything Ivy said on the video interviews a lie? Why hadn't Ivy ever said that nice stuff to Madison's face?

"*Your attention! Your attention, please!*" As Principal Bernard's voice boomed over the loudspeaker system, Ivy slipped her phone back into her bag. Everyone in the room stopped to listen.

"*Good morning, students. I am sad to announce that this morning we are saying good-bye to Mr. Lodge, Mrs. Finn, and their phenomenal film crew, who have been here at FHJH for a little more than a week. But we have a treat for you. After lunch, we will have a students-only screening of some rough footage from the interviews, during the main assembly. As a result, I am canceling the last two periods of the day so everyone may attend the screening. Of*

course, I expect your full cooperation in making this special event run smoothly. No running in the halls. No loud talking . . ."

As Principal Bernard spoke, a cheer rose up in the room. Madison heard the other seventh, eighth, and ninth graders yelling out and applauding in homerooms nearby.

"Hey, Maddie, I wonder if I made the video even though I was out sick," Egg wondered aloud. "Do you know? Did your mom tell you who made the cut?"

"No-o-o-o . . ." Madison grinned and shook her head.

It was a good question—and Madison realized she had no idea what Julian and Mom had chosen as the best of the best moments, even though she'd seen the B-reel at home.

Egg's question got her thinking (well, overthinking) all day: through Social Studies with Aimee; during a math pop quiz; and even during lunch. And by the time the last lunch bell finally rang, around one o'clock, she was still thinking about it.

"Let's go!" Aimee said, grabbing Madison's arm. They locked arms and headed for the assembly room with Lindsay, Fiona, and everyone else.

Principal Bernard's warnings to keep voices down didn't do much good. The room was noisier than noisy. Crowds of seventh, eighth, and ninth graders spoke and whistled at the tops of their lungs.

144

Anticipation for the screening was contagious. Even the teachers were in a flurry, talking about their own possible appearances on the film. Nothing like this had ever happened at FHJH before.

Madison hoped that she and Hart would sit near each other, but that wasn't how it worked out. She ended up in a seat between Dan and Lindsay instead.

After a brief introduction from Principal Bernard, Julian Lodge stepped up to the microphone.

Madison couldn't take her eyes off him. She replayed in her head the moment in Mom's office when she'd walked in on them in a clinch.

"He's still *such* a hottie," Lindsay said with a giggle.

Fiona and Aimee giggled, too, but Madison's face flushed.

This was the first time she'd really seen Julian in person since learning the whole truth about his relationship with Mom. It embarrassed her to hear the things her friends were saying. What would they say if they knew Madison's mom was dating the director? Wasn't that against the rules or something?

"Would you girls just shut up?" Egg said.

Now Madison giggled with relief. "Yeah, girls, let's stop talking about him like he's a movie star. He's just the director."

Aimee screwed up her nose and made a face at Madison. "What's gotten into you?" she asked. "I thought you liked Julian."

The lights in the auditorium dimmed. A few ninth graders let out a loud "Whoo! Whoo!"

The film began.

In truth, the rough cut was nothing more than a few scenes spliced together without making very much sense. But the film crew had captured some key, funny moments.

The opening scene panned across a classroom packed with eighth graders. Kids on screen spoke about the perils of being in junior high. As each person on screen talked, friends from the audience shrieked with laughter and excitement.

Next came a sequence of head shots set to music. Narration accompanying the shots of faces said, *"Junior high is a time to try new looks, new attitudes, and new friends."*

Up on the screen Madison saw Josh, a cute ninth grader, who also happened to be her next-door neighbor. She let out a little clap. It was hard to resist the urge to clap for *all* the faces. And Josh was extra special, even though he and Madison had been an item only in her dreams.

The loudest applause came when a familiar female face appeared.

"Look!" Egg cried. "It's Mariah!"

Madison smiled. Up on the screen, Egg's older sister Mariah's hair had been streaked pink at the edges. She'd highlighted it for the winter break; only some of it had washed out in the shower.

Mariah also wore several piercings, including eyebrow, nose, and ears. During school, piercings and heavy jewelry were not allowed, but after hours (or during a film shoot) exceptions were often made—and Mariah was one of them.

"What a freak!" Egg said, joking around. The real Mariah, seated ten rows ahead, whipped her head around.

"Watch it!" she cried.

Egg pretended that he hadn't heard his sister's slam, but of course he had. Egg always heard everything.

A musical interlude played over the quick succession of candid photos taken all over the school. As each photo appeared, the person in the picture would say, "That's me!" and the room would start laughing.

Ivy let out a squeal when she saw herself up there on screen. Her drones cheered, too. But Madison held her breath. What would Ivy say? Would her true confessions make the rough cut?

"I think the best parts of junior high are the cliques," Ivy said, flipping her red hair the way she always did when she was trying to be impressive. "I think exclusive groups are important. They give everyone something to aspire to."

Madison couldn't believe that out of all the nice things that had been said, *this* was the Ivy clip that Mom and Julian had chosen.

Close call.

Madison settled back into her chair.

Okay, this wasn't so bad at all.

As she watched, the screen split into four equal parts. Four boys' faces appeared. Hart's was one.

"Hey look, it's you!" Egg teased Hart. "I wish I had something to throw at the screen."

"Funny," Hart mumbled, his head in his hands.

Madison leaned around Lindsay and gave Hart a sidelong glance.

Don't worry. Madison mouthed the words and smiled broadly at him. *You look good.*

Hart smiled back. "Thanks, Finnster," he whispered.

"Oh, my God," Fiona blurted out. "Look!"

Madison snapped her attention back to the film. Up on the screen she saw a very different scene now: Fiona and her teammates taking to the soccer field. The narrator read off some facts about sports and teenagers while the camera moved in slow motion over Fiona's hands and knees and up to her face. She had a determined look on her face, the way she always did before performing penalty kicks.

"I can't believe they're going to show you missing that kick," Aimee said.

"I know!" Fiona covered her eyes. "Don't look!"

"No, look!" Madison cried. She pointed up to the screen.

Madison knew Mom wouldn't embarrass Fiona. She remembered back to the day at the field. Julian

148

had been so determined to get the right shot. But he hadn't cared at all about whether or not the soccer ball had flown into the goal net. He had cared only about the anticipation, the sweat, and the hard, hard work. *That* was what he'd hoped to capture on the film.

Egg wasn't saying much now. He gazed up at the screen, moon pie–eyed and proud. Fiona looked beautiful up there, getting ready to make her big kick. She looked like the stars she loved, like Mia Hamm and all the rest.

All at once, the screen dissolved into another shot, of kids playing basketball. Chet was on camera a little bit, catching a ball and making a pass. Egg teased him about it just as he'd teased everyone else (except Fiona, of course).

Swiftly the film moved into the FHJH ice hockey arena. The camera swirled around a bunch of eighth and ninth graders on the hockey team as they skated and bucked the sideboards and shot pucks into the net. Then the camera pulled back and panned across the bench.

Egg sat on the end, staring off into space.

"It isn't whether you win or lose. It's how you play the game," the narrator's voice said. *"If you play the game."*

Madison let out a little laugh. Lindsay laughed, too. Pretty soon, everyone in their row was doubled over.

"That's the footage of me that they showed?" Egg complained. "Aw, Maddie, you have to get your mom to pull that out. Please."

Madison kept right on laughing. No one felt too bad for Egg. After all, he'd opened his own big mouth one too many times. It served him right.

More scenes followed from the halls of school.

"In addition to heavy class work," the narrator continued, *"the students at Far Hills Junior High take their responsibilities outside the classroom very seriously."*

The camera focused on a group of ninth-grade candy stripers who volunteered at the local hospital. Then it showed a few kids and teachers planting seedlings up in the school's greenhouse. Finally, it showed a litter of new puppies.

"Oh, no," Madison said.

The camera zoomed in on the litter and then pulled back. Madison was leaning over, smiling. Dan stood behind her, his hands on Madison's shoulders. They were laughing together.

Dan nudged Madison. "Hey, it's us. Trippy, right?"

Madison couldn't sink any lower in her seat. She could feel Aimee's eyes, Fiona's eyes, Egg's eyes—everyone's eyes—on her.

"Trippy," she said to Dan.

Madison glanced over at Hart, expecting the same kind of reassurance she'd given him.

But Hart wasn't looking at her. He stared straight ahead at the screen, eyes fixed on Madison and Dan, who were still sharing a good laugh.

"Pretty dumb, huh?" Madison said, trying to get Hart's attention.

He looked over and shrugged. "You bet," he said. Then he turned to Chet, who was sitting on the other side of him.

Lindsay leaned into Madison. "What's *his* problem?" she asked softly.

"He's just being goofy," Madison said, trying to laugh it off.

By now, the film had split into equal parts again. First it was split in half and then into fours and then into sixteen little squares. Each square contained the face of one of the students. The cubes got smaller and smaller still, until they were little gingham dots representing the bulk of the student body at FHJH.

Background music played as the lights came up in the auditorium.

Chet and Egg gave each other a high five for being stars, even though Fiona joked that they were only "stars in their own little minds."

When Madison looked over a third time at Hart, he was still not speaking to her—or anyone else. Now Madison was beginning to worry.

"Um . . . Hart?" Madison whispered, hoping to get Hart's attention.

Principal Bernard leaned into the microphone up

onstage and told everyone in the assembly room that they were dismissed. Teachers helped students exit the room and head for their lockers in an orderly fashion.

Madison tried catching up with Hart on the way out.

"Hold up!" she said, tagging his shoulder. "What did you think?"

"I didn't know you and Dan were hanging out," Hart mumbled.

"Hanging out?" Madison asked. "That was just at the clinic," she said.

"Yeah, sure . . ." Hart said.

"Really, we're just friends, Hart," Madison said. "You know that."

"I guess," Hart said. He pushed ahead slightly into a crowd of kids and Madison lost sight of him.

"Maddie!" Aimee grabbed Madison's arm. "Wait for us."

Fiona was right behind her. "Hart looks mad. What's up?"

"He's acting weird about the video. I don't know why," Madison said.

Lindsay joined the cluster of BFFs, a big smile on her face.

"Aw, Hart's just jealous," Aimee said. "I was watching him watching the video," she said.

"This is like a soap opera," Madison said. "I didn't do anything wrong. Why is he mad at me?"

"Not mad, Maddie," Aimee said. "Jealous. There's a big difference."

"Well you *were* touching Dan," Lindsay grumbled.

"What?" Madison asked.

"I think the whole scene is a good sign," Fiona said.

"What's good about it?" Madison inquired.

"This is a sign that Hart likes you," Aimee added.

"Um . . . where's the sign that Dan likes me?" Lindsay asks aloud.

Madison, Aimee, and Fiona shot her a look.

Then the four of them burst into laughter.

Chapter 13

Madison dumped her orange messenger bag on to the kitchen table at home on Monday night. Her favorite pen rolled onto the floor. She sifted through scraps of paper, including a bright yellow flyer that she'd ripped off her locker before coming home.

It's a Wrap Breakfast
Come Say Thank You and Good-bye
to the Film Crew
Far Hills Junior High School Cafeteria
Tuesday Morning
7:30–8:30 AM

Mom strolled into the kitchen carrying a pile of papers.

"You're home!" Mom said. "I'm sorry I missed the

premiere at school today. We're under such a tight deadline. Julian needed me to continue viewing the B-reel. The rough cut you saw was really just thrown together. We have so much work left to do. . . ."

"It was good, Mom," Madison conceded. "Really good. I liked it."

Mom grinned. "Really good? Well, gee, that's like an Academy Award nomination, coming from you."

"Ha-ha, very funny," Madison said.

"No, I'm pleased that you liked what you saw. Even the part with you on film?" Mom asked cautiously.

"Even the part with me," Madison said.

"Good," Mom said.

Madison reached out to take Mom's arm, but the pile of papers slid through Mom's hands and fell on the floor.

"Oh, no!" Mom cried. "I just spent an hour putting those time-code sheets in order."

"I'm sorry," Madison blurted. "I just . . ."

Mom was on her hands and knees. "This project has turned into a headache in more ways than one, I swear. . . ."

Madison stood back, surprised at Mom's admission.

"What do you mean? You just said it was good . . ." Madison said.

"Oh, Maddie, I just have a lot on my plate," Mom replied.

"You mean Julian?" Madison asked.

"Julian? Hardly. We never talk about anything but work."

"Um . . . Mom . . . I was wondering . . . if . . . can you take off a little time tonight and just hang out with me?" Madison asked. "I really feel like talking."

"Oh, honey bear, tonight? There's just no way," Mom said. "I have too much to do right now. And now these papers . . . what a mess. Can it wait?"

Mom scrambled to grab at the papers and shuffle them into new piles.

"Well, I guess I'll go do homework or something then," Madison said.

"Yes, you go ahead and do that," Mom said. "I'll be in my office."

Madison walked away.

"In your office," she said under her breath. "What a surprise."

Upstairs, Madison turned again to her laptop.

At least *it* had time for Madison tonight.

She logged on, searching to see if her keypal was logged on, too. For some reason, her Insta-Message to Bigwheels came back "undeliverable."

Madison went into her files.

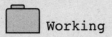 Working

Rude Awakening: Mom's always, ALWAYS working. So how come my relationship with her isn't?

This is such old news, but for the first time I actually feel jilted. I've spent the last week or so stressing about Mom and the video and Julian and her dating and EVERYTHING. And today I finally get it. I get what she's doing with these movies. I see that maybe Julian isn't such a bad guy. But when I try to let Mom know that for once I really DO get it, she says she's too busy to talk and off to her office she goes.

I HATE HATE HATE THAT!!!

Not to mention the fact that Bigwheels is MIA. (Hmmmm. I wonder: is EVERYONE running away from me? First Mom, then Hart, and now my keypal, too? Argh!) Something is always up when Bigwheels doesn't answer e-mail. I'm so sure she's off chatting with Melody. :>P

Maybe I need to get my very own class pal. That'll show Bigwheels that she's not the only one who

Madison's computer dinged. An Insta-Message popped up.

<Bigwheels>: Hey did u just send me an I-M

Madison let out a little gasp. She curled her feet up underneath her and started typing madly on the keyboard.

\<MadFinn\>: OMG you must be psychic
I was just thinking that you blew
me off again

\<Bigwheels\>: WAYTA?

\<MadFinn\>: Well u never wrote back

\<Bigwheels\>: when?

\<MadFinn\>: yesterday

\<Bigwheels\>: ur crazy I totally
wrote back I would never BLOW you
off

\<MadFinn\>: oh

\<Bigwheels\>: r u ok?

\<MadFinn\>: how's yr class pal Melody

\<Bigwheels\>: oh, we had our last
e-mail on Friday this week they
have tests in Australia

\<MadFinn\>: so? Yr keypals. can't she
write 2 u n e way??

\<Bigwheels\>: NR it's a classroom
e-mail and we didn't exchange
home e-mails u know 4 safety

\<MadFinn\>: really?

\<Bigwheels\>: the teachers wanted
it to be in the classroom only
4 now

\<MadFinn\>: but u want melody's home
e-mail don't you?

\<Bigwheels\>: I guess but I already
have a keypal so it's no biggie
:>)))

\<MadFinn\>: you mean me?

```
<Bigwheels>: OC what do u think?
<MadFinn>: :>)))
<Bigwheels>: melody was nice but we
  talked mostly about school and
  after school not like us
<MadFinn>: whoa I thought melody was
  like ur new BOFF
<Bigwheels>: NW! that's U maddie :>)
<MadFinn>: even if I'm not
  international?
<Bigwheels>: Wha? u live in New
  York that's pretty cool
<MadFinn>: yeah, I guess
<Bigwheels>: so . . . tell me how's
  HART
<MadFinn>: Loooooong story
<Bigwheels>: ok spill it
```

Madison kept typing, faster and faster, until she started making all sorts of spelling mistakes. There was so much to say, so much to share.

Bigwheels was back.

The wrap party on Tuesday at school wasn't at all what Madison expected.

For starters, Julian and the rest of the film crew didn't really mingle with the other students. Principal Bernard had positioned them apart so they could talk to some important official from the mayor's office that came by to "observe" the festivities and screen the rough cut. A local reporter was there, too, writing a short piece about the documentary's "message."

Despite the groups of kids pushing forward and backward, Madison hoped that maybe she'd shove into the pack for her chance to speak to—and thank—Julian. She really needed to apologize for being cranky during the filming. But no matter how hard Madison tried to inch closer to Julian, she felt as if she were standing still.

After about twenty minutes of the students' talking among themselves, Principal Bernard grabbed a portable mike and got everyone's attention.

"Attention, students," Principal Bernard said quickly. "We need to wrap this up. So, if you would please put your hands together and let Mr. Lodge and the others know what a terrific time we've had . . ."

The kids clapped.

Julian leaned into the mike, too, and quickly added, "Let's not Forget Francine Finn. Without her, this project would not be happening."

Madison gasped as Mom appeared at a side door, on cue, scarves wrapped around her neck, chunky brown earrings on. She waved hello to the room and then started clapping herself.

Students clapped furiously. Even Egg went "Woo! Woo!" with his fist in the air.

Mom looked pleased with herself. She didn't look

the least bit harried or distracted, the way she'd looked the night before.

Madison wanted to run away. She couldn't watch this. She couldn't be here. Mom had complained of having all that work the previous night, too much work to talk to her own daughter; and yet here she was, taking a proper break, available to everyone else.

Hmmm.

"Your mom looks pretty today," Lindsay whispered in Madison's ear.

Madison nodded politely, because she was afraid that if she tried to speak she would get emotional. And if she got emotional, then Egg would poke fun at her, and even her friends would laugh, and then everyone else in the school would stare and stare. . . .

"Finnster?"

Madison turned around. Hart was right there, practically touching her arm, his nose just inches away from hers.

"Hey," Madison mumbled.

"Hey," Hart said.

"Lame party, right?" Madison asked.

"Maddie? I'm sorry I acted like a jerk."

"When?" Madison asked coyly.

Hart laughed. "You know what I'm talking about."

"You mean yesterday?"

Hart nodded.

"Aimee said you were just being jealous," Madison stated matter-of-factly.

Hart's eyes bugged out wide. "Um . . . I don't think . . ."

"Are you?" Madison asked.

"M—m—maybe I am, a little bit," Hart stammered. "Well. Sort of. I mean, we did say that we were kind of . . . well, I guess we didn't say what we were exactly, but . . ."

"It's okay," Madison said. "I get it. You don't have to say any more."

"Thanks," Hart said quietly.

"Yeah," Madison said.

Since they were standing in the middle of the crowded school cafeteria, Madison couldn't hold his hand. So she just stared at it.

Hart's long fingers drummed against his thigh. He looked up at the ceiling.

And then he looked right at Madison's face, into her eyes.

The clapping continued around them. Mom was making a little speech now. But Madison wasn't listening to or watching anyone but Hart.

In the history of moments between them, this surely was one Madison would never forget.

Chapter 14

From: MadFinn
To: Bigwheels
Subject: PALS
Date: Wed 2 Feb 3:58 PM

1st: I haven't been a VG keypal l8ly. Sorry 4 that.

2nd: I miss you.

3rd: You're always asking about Hart and now I can finally say that HJ is gr8er than gr8! Yesterday we were standing together in the lunchroom @ school and it felt like those five minutes of nice time with him wiped out the entire drama of the last week or so.

Thanks 4 saying all that stuff u
said about being my keypal b4 u
were n e one else's. I have to
admit that I was a little jealous
I guess b/c I wished u were writing
2 me every day and not her. But I
C now how class pals and keypals
are way different. I checked out
those links to those other cool
Web sites, esp. the one that talks
about Pet Pals. I really had no
idea that there were so many
different kinds of online friends. I
couldn't believe there were people
who wrote e-mails back and forth
about things like collecting stamps
or baking cakes.

Well, I have 2 go finish a problem
set now.

Yours till the cell phones,

MadFinn

The laptop snapped shut as Madison opened her
math textbook and sprawled across her bed. She'd
already started to work on the problem set in study
hall but hadn't gotten very far.

Madison tried to collect her thoughts.

Inside the house, the boiler hummed loudly. Off

in the distance outside her window, she heard the faint trill of small birds, probably searching for the sunflower seeds Mom had loaded into the bird feeder near the porch. And somewhere in the background, she heard a low thump, probably coming from someone's souped-up car stereo as the person drove around with the volume at full blast.

Then Madison heard footsteps.

Within moments, Mom was at the door. Phin trailed behind her, his little pug nose sniffing the carpet.

Madison expected some kind of confrontation. All week long, it had seemed as though every time Mom came to collect her daughter from the upstairs bedroom, Madison had locked the door to keep Mom out.

But today was different. Today, the door remained open.

So what was on Mom's mind? She stood with her back to the door, arms crossed in front of her.

"Mom?" Madison asked. Usually when Mom stood that way it meant that she was upset. "Um . . . are you okay?"

Mom wiped her nose. She bent and lifted Phin into her arms.

"Come with me," Mom said, turning back to the staircase.

Madison followed her downstairs.

"Mom, what is this? Is something wrong?"

Madison asked. Her imagination buzzed. Had something happened between Mom and Julian? Had they broken up? Was Julian downstairs right now?

Once downstairs, Madison realized that no one else was there. It was just the three of them, as usual.

Mom solemnly led Madison into her office.

"Sit down," Mom said.

"Okay, Mom, you're freaking me out a little bit," Madison said. "I mean . . . can't you tell me what this is. Are you mad? I know I've been a pain this week, but I thought we talked about that and . . ."

"Shhhh," Mom said gently. She turned on one of her video monitors.

The image of Julian Lodge filled the screen.

Madison sighed.

This was about Julian.

But Mom lurched forward and hit the fast-forward button. "Hold on," she said, pausing the machine after only a few seconds. "I want you to see this."

Madison's stomach was in knots by now. She could only imagine what video clip Mom had unearthed from the hours of footage from the previous week. Was it the interview with Ivy admitting how much she missed Maddie? Was it mystery footage of Hart admitting how much he liked Maddie? It was fun to think about all the possibilities.

Mom clicked PLAY, and the DVD/VCR started to roll footage of someone else entirely.

On the screen now was Madison, sitting in a blue chair, in the middle of the media lab, talking to the camera while someone in the background asked her questions.

Madison cringed.

Her skin looked a little orange. She should have listened when Ivy had suggested that she put on a little lip gloss.

"Junior high is only hard sometimes, like when I can't do a science project because my partner is . . . well, I don't want to say anything bad about anyone on video."

The interviewer laughed.

"What are the hardest challenges facing you in junior high?" he asked.

On the screen, Madison looked up, then to the side, then straight at the camera.

"Well, let's see. We're being really honest, right? Okay, here it goes. My parents . . . they got divorced last year and . . . well, my mom has this real important job. But . . . um . . . I think everyone here knows her, actually . . . Where was I? Yes, well . . . Sometimes I think she decided that she needed to work twice as hard when she and my dad split up. He does the same thing . . . and that usually means . . . "

Madison scrunched down into the chair in Mom's office as she watched the video clip. She'd forgotten all about saying those things.

"A lot of my friends have the same problem. Junior high is like this weird time because you don't really want to be around your parents at all. But then . . . like with Mom . . . when my parents aren't around . . . it's hard. I have to admit that I miss them. And I just wish . . . well . . . I just wish Mom didn't have to work so much. . . ."

Madison looked away from the video toward Mom.

But Mom's eyes remained locked on the video.

"I think now that parents have to work so hard, they figure their kids won't mind if they aren't around. But sometimes the opposite is true. At least for me it is. And this year that's been the hardest. Well, that and dealing with my enemies and pop quizzes and not exactly being in the popular crowd. The usual drama, you know . . ."

Mom grabbed the arm of her chair and shot Madison a long look.

"Mom, are you crying?" Madison asked.

"No," Mom said, shaking off her emotion. "No. I know that would embarrass you."

"It's not a big deal if you cry," Madison said. "But it's really no big thing, the video. I mean, people say things all the time. . . ."

Madison stared at her sneakers rather than looking over at Mom again.

"Late last night when I told you I had so much work to finish up," Mom said, "I was sitting down here, time-coding some new pieces. I found this clip when I was on one of the B-reels."

"Yeah," Madison said, eyes still on the floor.

"Well, Maddie, I thought you told me that you hadn't done an interview."

"I didn't do one. Not at first," Madison said. "But then at the very last minute Aimee and Fiona and Lindsay talked me into it."

"They did? How?"

"They said I should do it for you," Madison said.

Mom laughed. She was visibly choked up. "Oh, Maddie," Mom said. She stood up and grabbed Madison by the shoulders. "You are really something."

"Something what?" Madison asked. "That doesn't necessarily mean something good, does it?"

Mom laughed again, apparently so she wouldn't cry. "Of course it means something good," Mom said.

"Whew," Madison said with a little smile. "I was worried."

"Honey bear," Mom asked. "Why didn't you tell me what you were feeling? Have you always disliked my work?"

"I don't dislike your work," Madison said. "I think your job is one of the coolest on the planet. Really . . ."

"You told me this before, didn't you?" Mom finally asked. "Earlier this week. You said you

169

needed to talk and I was too—" Mom caught her breath. "I was too busy working on this, wasn't I?" Mom asked.

"I guess so," Madison said.

Mom slumped back into one of her office chairs.

"I feel so stupid," Mom said. "I've been so caught up in the project that I missed all the important things, like time with you. What's wrong with me?"

Madison shrugged. "It's okay, Mom."

Mom sighed. "I feel like I am always playing catch-up."

"You'll get caught up someday, won't you?" Madison asked.

Mom stood up and took Madison by the arm, lifting Madison out of her own seat.

"Come with me," Mom said.

"Again?" Madison asked. "What now?"

Mom stopped in the middle of the room. She opened her arms wide and then wrapped them around Madison's middle.

"Maddie," Mom whispered into Madison's left ear. "I will never forget this week, Madison. I will never forget the film shoot at your school."

Madison closed her eyes. Mom's breath felt warm. She smelled liked citrus. Madison thought that she could feel Mom's heart, beating hard.

"And I will never, ever forget any of the special things you've said," Mom said.

As she heard those words, Madison's legs

wobbled a little. She hugged Mom back, and her body went limp as a noodle.

As Madison and Mom embraced, however, someone else nuzzled in on the action. Someone furry.

Phin bit into the leg of Madison's jeans and tugged.

"Oh, Phinnie!" Madison cried. "We haven't forgotten you, either!"

Mom smiled and turned off her film equipment, and the three of them stepped into the kitchen to have a real, homemade dinner.

Mad Chat Words:

2C4W	Too cool (or, cute) for words
Sked	Schedule
NR	Not really
CSS>)	Can't stop smiling
SO&T	Stay online and talk
Hrs	Hours
POV	Point of view
WTBD	What's the big deal?
ONOOO	Oh, nooo
8>}	I'm losing my mind
DRA	Don't run away
((Heart))	Totally love it more than anything
Wk	Week
VVC	Very, very cool
WBSTS	Write back sooner than soon

<u>Madison's Computer Tip</u>

Bigwheels freaked me out when she said she had a new keypal. Of course, my worries were groundless. Her relationship with an international class pal wasn't anything like her relationship with me. **Online relationships are not created equal. Some pals are for today. Some pals are forever.** I thought Bigwheels had thrown me over for another online pal in Australia, but she hadn't. Melody was only a pal during school. It takes a long time online to really and truly get to know someone.

For a complete Mad Chat dictionary and more about Madison Finn, visit Madison at www.lauradower.com